Sensual Indian

Sensual Indian

(Novella)

Jani Zirakpuria

AuthorHouse™
1663 Liberty Drive
Bloomington, IN 47403
www.authorhouse.com
Phone: 1-800-839-8640

First published by AuthorHouse 07/06/2011

ISBN: 978-1-4567-8297-9 (sc)

Library of Congress Control Number: 2011909585

Printed in the United States of America

All the characters in this novella are based on fantasy and the resemblance with anybody if any may be unintentional.

This book is printed on acid-free paper.

DEDICATION

To the eternal female of the human specie for fascinating man to live on this otherwise drab and problematic planet earth.

Thankfulness

The writer is profusely thankful to the following sources of inspiration, for enthusing him with self-confidence and courage of conviction enough, to give written shape to his thought process :

1. Gurbux Singh Preet Lari
2. Khushwant Singh
3. Mohinder Singh Walia
4. Darshan Singh Maini
5. Dr. Romesh Kuntal Megh
6. Prof. Phul Chand 'Manav'
7. Sasthi Brata
8. Vimla Patil
9. Yogesh Snehi
10. Prof. Yashpal
11. Dr. Stephen Hawking
12. Nicolaus Copernicus
13. Giordano Bruno
14. Galileo
15. Isaac Newton
16. Sigmund Freud
17. Preet Lari (Monthly)
18. Tarksheel (Monthly)
19. Reader's Digest (Monthly)
20. India Today (Weekly)
21. The Tribune (Daily)
22. The Indian Express (Daily)
23. Hindustan Times (Daily)
24. Ajit (Daily)

25. Desh Sewak (Daily)
26. Punjab Kesri (Daily)
27. Amar Ujala (Daily)
28. Dainik Bhasker (Daily)

Glossary of Indian words used in 'Sensual Indian'

Ajanta	A place known for its stone-carved cave-temples in India
Arti	A ritual of Hindu way of worship
Ashta-dhatu	Eight-metal alloy
Avatar	Form, guise, personification, birth
Babu	An official
Bartan	Utensil
Bartanwali	The woman who cleans utensils (bartans) door-to—door
Bhagwa	Saffron
Bhangra	A world famous Punjabi dance
Bindi	A colourful object pasted on the forehead by married women
Bukky	Mount (mare) of Mirza, the lover of Sahiban
Chadra	Flowing cloth to wrap the lower body of a person as in Punjab
Chela	Disciple
Chola	Gown
Choli	Blouse
Devta	Deity
Dhoti	A flowing cloth to wrap the lower body of a person
Lungi	A flowing cloth to wrap the lower body of a person
Didi	Respectful mode of address for elder sister
Dum dum deega	Opening line of a Hindi film song denoting happiness
Dupatta	Flowing cloth used as head cover by Punjabi women

Feri	Visit
Ghagra	An ankle length skirt with numerous folds
Ghungat	Covering of face by women with the odhni / dupatta
Ghungat uthai	Lifting of face cover of the married woman
Gorra chitta	Fair complexion
Gorree chittee	Fair complexioned woman
Grara	An ankle length skirt
Guchha	Bunch
Guru	Teacher
Gut nagni	Snake like plait of hair
Hindi	National language of India
Jagrata	Nightlong singing of devotional songs
Jalebi Joora	Hair tied in a round knot
Janam kundli	A document detailing course of a person's life
Jijaji	Sister's husband
Kabab ki haddi	Something obnoxious spoiling the taste
Kachhi	Underwear
Kajufeni	Liquor made from 'kaju' (a dry fruit) in Kerala
Kamasutra	The ancient Indian treatise on the art of lovemaking
Kameez	Shirt
Kangra	Name of a place known for a particular type of paintings
Kanya	Girl
Khajuraho	Name of a place known for stone-carved cave—temples
Koka	An ornament for nose
Lungi	A flowing cloth to wrap the lower body of a person

Mahendi	A plant based dye to colour hands and feet for decoration
Mangal Sutra	A pendant worn by married woman
Mantra	Recitation
Moun	Silence
Mukut	Crown
Munni	Baby girl
Odhni	A loose flowing cloth used as head cover by women
Paan	A chewing concoction
Pallu	A portion of 'sari' used as head cover
Pandav	Five brothers in epic Mahabharat
Patiala-peg	A heavy peg of liquor as they drink in Patiala
Pranda	A contraption of threads to plait the hair
Prantha	A form of bread soaked in fat
Prasadam	Sweetmeats etc. distributed among devotees
Puja	Worship
Pujari	Priest
Punjaban	A woman from Punjab
Purnima	Full moon
Puttra	Son
Raja	King
Salwar	Woman's trousers as they use in Punjab
Sapna	Dream
Sari	A flowing cloth as Indian women's mode of dress
Sati	Custom of voluntary or forcible burning of woman alive in the funeral pyre of her husband
Shankracharya	A religious authority
Shagun	Gift of money in celebration

Shavasan	Corpse pose
Sifarish	Recommendation for help
Somras	Liquor (As mentioned in ancient Indian texts).
Suhagraat	First night of married life
Tadka	Mixing of fat and spices with the curries etc. by heating
Tan, man, dhan	Body, mind and material possessions
Thakur	A person belonging to a Rajput clan.
Thali	A plate like utensil
Tilk	Mark of sandalwood paste on the forehead made by Hindus
Tirtha	Place of pilgrimage
Yagna	An elaborate ritual of Hinduism aimed at pleasing Gods
Yakshini	Woman symbol of the stone-carved cave-temples

Chapter 1

On the second look, he could not take his eyes off the 'feast' and sank into a chair! Wide-eyed!! Watching!!!

The beauty under shower had already soaped her chiselled granite body, and was slowly rubbing it. She was taking slow turns, left and right, to ensure proper wash. As she turned and twisted under the falling water, he could clearly see her hands; moving on her hips and narrow waist, and then cupping the lovely pair of breasts and alternately bringing the two honey pots under direct shower.

"... Vow ... !"

"... What a view ... !"

"... Par excellence ... !"

"... Water melting from a nude virgin's face and shoulders ... !"

"... Down to the lovely breasts, belly-button, pubic-pad, and the hidden love-pot ... !"

"... And cascading over the corpulent hips and shapely thighs to the floor below ... !"

"... Making sounds like muffled jingle-bells ... !"

"... Unpolluted beauty ... !"

"... A blooming flower ... !"

"... Nature at its best ... !"

". . . What a shape . . . !"

". . . An 'ashta-dhatu' idol . . . !"

". . . Vibrating and pulsating . . . !"

". . . In flesh and blood . . . !"

". . . Lavishly handsome . . . !"

". . . Tantalizing, titillating, and tempting . . . !"

". . . Mesmerizing . . . !"

". . . What a total transformation from what I had seen seven years back . . . !"

"Oh . . . ! Oh . . . !"

". . . ! . . !"

While he was watching wonderstruck with his consciousness crowded with amorous thoughts like a pit of snakes, the view was suddenly lost to him.

Oh! It vanished as quickly as it had emerged!

Because, sensing his presence, the beauty in the bath gave him a sheepish look, and snap-closed the bathroom door!

No doubt, her action was the one expected from an average Indian girl of her age and upbringing. Yet an idea took shape in his mind, with possibility of one day transforming into action!

The idea?

Yes, the idea!

The idea was . . . !

* * *

Chapter 2

Seven years before the bathroom incident, she was merely an eleven-year old fledgling of a girl. With cast-iron complexion, she was insect-thin and three-and-a-half-feet in height. Her eyes were sunken due to mal-nutrition. The cobweb of her hair seemed to have never experienced a comb. She wore an outsized and much faded T-shirt, almost competing in length with her black rag of a skirt, and her rickety legs stood on untidy bare feet.

'Is she not a mockery of a girl? Just simulation? Pretension? Derision? Misrepresentation? Distortion? Imitation? Or all-in-one?' With such epithets competing with each other in his mind like participants of a marathon race, he decided on 'parody', which he felt should be her name. That was, if ever the names were to describe the people.

Well, seven years before the bathroom incident, Parody had come to his house trailing her elder sister, probably as an escort. Thirty-one year old, five feet and four inches in height and granite-complexioned, her elder sister had come to negotiate wages as part-time domestic worker, they call 'bartanwali' in North India. The job was upkeep of his house on day-to-day basis.

He was then living as a 'forced bachelor' in the thirty-second year of his age, in a fourth-floor flat, located in the posh area of a state capital in South India, very far from his native Punjab. He had gone there on a 'punishment posting' given by a whimsical senior of the flourishing Public Sector Undertaking, in which he was employed as a middle rung executive. His wife had decided to stay back, to safeguard their interests in the joint-family ventures. It was also to look after the two school-going brats sired by him, whose bringing up could have been a problem down south, with people speaking unknown languages and wearing 'strange looking' clothes.

There were not many takers for the part-time domestic's job, with a Punjabi living as a forced bachelor in that distant land. So, he readily agreed to pay the exorbitant wages demanded by the 'bartanwali'. She was also to get weekly off on Sunday, the day of worship in that area. He knew, the wages of part-time domestics were meagre in that part of India, but, his need was paramount, and also he wanted to avoid frequent change of hands. The ploy really paid off, and the 'bartanwali' took to the job immediately.

In fact he did not have many demands in the matters of the three basic jobs entrusted to the 'bartanwali' as his part-time domestic worker. There was nothing much for her to do in the name of house cleaning, as he used only balcony, bedroom, lobby and the kitchen; keeping the other three rooms almost closed. The dishwashing was not much of a job, as he often did it himself as well when required, and the washing of clothes was also no problem.

Also, being an introvert, he did not make any friends on official and social levels, and no guests ever came from the distant Punjab. So, there were usually no visitors to his house and thus he had entirely to him, all his spare time including weekends and other holidays. In addition, he was usually able to skip office on some afternoons on will. That was under various pretexts, as akin to most of us, Indians.

He usually spent the spare time in his house; reading, writing or watching television. No doubt, as a health freak he regularly went for morning walk, and practiced yoga and acupressure.

For sure, he never bothered to find faults in 'bartanwali''s work, and nor did he ever scold her for skipping a day or two due to various reasons including her 'monthly periods'. He paid her regularly even for no work, when he visited his family in Punjab on leave; at least twice every year.

Thus, the arrangement worked without any hassles for long. Also in its wake came many surprises, giving him a peep into the working of human mind, which can be wonderfully motivated to lead the human being to survival, in the face of adversity. Yes! For sure!!

* * *

Chapter 3

As 'bartanwali' took up the job, both of them abstained from talking to each other beyond the usual exchange of hand-folded 'Namaskar', submissive mode of greetings, for some days in the beginning. It was overtly due to difference in status. Covertly, perhaps it was an attempt; on his part, to present himself as a no-nonsense-type of person, and on her, the average Indian woman's show of vanity-cum-shyness.

Then she reluctantly took to accepting tea or coffee offered by him. Some time in her smattering of Hindi, the national language of India, she also spoke of what could best be described as cautions being thrown to her by other domestics of her genre, against working for a lonely-living 'outsider' and that too a burly Punjabi, that he was.

However, finding him as a no-nonsense-type, her confidence increased, and one fine day she offered to make his coffee. She also prepared a heavy omelette at his instance, and partook half of it with coffee.

Then she took to bringing from her home, some local delicacies off and on, which she claimed to have specially prepared for him.

With the days rolling into weeks and months, 'bartanwali' thus went on shedding her shyness and fear, ultimately becoming bold enough, not to even hesitate taking a shower in his attached bathroom after machine-washing his clothes.

In due course, 'bartanwali' also told him that her husband was a factory hand, who being a drunkard was of no significant financial help to the family. Her immediate family, besides her younger sister, included her mother and the aged parents of her husband; all unfit to earn their upkeep. Her son had dropped out of primary school and was working as a domestic in far away Delhi. However, he never sent any financial help to the family, which lived in a congested locality on the edge of the sprawling posh area. A daughter born to her had died at the age of four and her sister and mother were living with her, because they had nowhere to go. That was due to the untimely demise of her father in a road accident wherein her mother had become a cripple. She had an elder sister; married and settled at Delhi, but not financially well off.

One thing, which he took some days to notice about 'bartanwali', she was not flabby type. Her bosom was in a very good shape despite having suckled two off springs, and there was an appreciable degree of flexibility in her figure. Her body reflexes were very quick, and she went about her work with the precision of a machine and the quickness of a cat. No doubt, all this had come to her from the physical exercise she was inadvertently taking in her day-to-day domestic jobs, whereby she had to constantly go upstairs, sit, stand, bend, twist, stretch, lift weights, and push and pull objects; synchronizing the powers of her mind and body. So, being 'fit like a fiddle', she never complained of headache, giddiness, joint pains, nausea and breathlessness, which generally haunt the average Indian woman at her age.

With her hourglass figure, she was a desirably well-proportioned female of the human specie. An exceptional replica of 'Yakshini' of the stone-carved

Khajuraho cave-temples of Madhya Pradesh! A perfect sex symbol as envisaged in Kamasutra: the ancient Indian treatise on the art of lovemaking! Short-stature, bulging breasts, exceptionally thin waist, protruding hips and ample thighs! Since his visit to Khajuraho as a college student, he had been chasing such beauties only in dream: 'Sapna'. No wonder he named 'bartanwali' as Sapna in his heart of hearts, though her real name was 'Roop Mala', which literally means 'garland of beauty'.

The main complaint Sapna had from life was about the drunken behaviour of her husband, whom she described as a nincompoop nonentity and a spent-force, having no interest in her and the family. Speaking about her husband, she often took to sobbing and held him responsible for her misfortune of going door-to-door as a domestic worker.

On such occasions, when Sapna opened her mind about personal problems, he sympathized with her lavishly and prompted her to continue the struggle of life with determination.

"You see the life comes only once. Why take it lying down?" he said. He told her, "Like rivers and the seas, there are also up and low tides in the lives of humans, who should face the resulting situations boldly, instead of submitting to the vagaries of the so-called fate, which is certainly the refuge of those who are mentally weak. Constant and slow change is the law of nature, which actually makes the things work. As the day replaces night and summer replaces winter regularly, so for sure, the good and bad phases replace each other in human life, though the duration may vary from person to person, which is also the same for families, communities, countries or whatever socio-political groups are formed by humans. Furthermore, the human being is the most intelligent of all forms of life on this planet earth, no doubt still in the developing stage. Why should this most intelligent creature live miserably, is the question, which we should always keep in mind. With this realisation comes the zest to live. And to live zestfully with self respect and happiness, we should be able to mould the circumstances of life as per our basic requirements, without of course infringing upon the genuine rights of others".

He further told her, "Every human being is full of countless possibilities with the potential of developing into favourable realities. The need on our part is only to have determination enough to translate the possibility into reality. More determined we are to change our life for the better, more successful we will be at it. If you think your life would be changed for the better by what you call God, take my word you are mistaken. I dare say, it is only your mindset, which can help you change your life for the better, and for that, you need to change your mindset from helplessness and frustration to optimism and determination. Do not just waste your time and energy on cursing your life for what you do not have. Just make proper use of your sense of reasoning, to take the best out of what you have. Never weep over what you call your 'bad luck'. Always strive to change the situation to your liking. The best way to make a beginning is by following what they say: If you do not have what you like, you should like what you have. So, with this in mind, instead of cursing your so-called stars and waiting for the so-called God for help, you should concentrate on building the blocks of better life with what you have".

"Furthermore, the best of the resources available to us is our mind, which is empowered to dream and plan. To be successful at fruitful dreaming and planning, we should see our life in three modes: past, present, and future. We know, the 'past' is the time gone by, which never comes back. As they say 'It is useless to cry over spilt milk', so it is useless to worry about what we could not achieve during the life gone by. The 'future' is a mystery, which only keeps us in wait. So, why bother about something of which we are not yet sure. The only available mode of life with us is the 'present', which in real sense is the gift of life. So, to enjoy this gift of life, we should only concentrate on the 'present mode', which is available to us. This, we can do by making the best use of our available possessions and not bothering about what we do not have. By doing so, we can, not only turn our past life into a store-house of happy memories with the passage of time, but also plan to make proper use of the future. To begin with, we only need to stimulate our mind with 'attention towards what is available to us', accompanied by 'intention' of making its proper use for our happiness. And once you make a beginning with a positive mindset, the sky is the limit I tell you!"

Hammered into her mind repeatedly with personal touch and sympathetic approach, his ideas gave Sapna courage and grit to face and enjoy life in its 'present mode'. So, finding a well-wisher in him, she perhaps felt drawn towards him, exhibiting an urge to benefit from his guiding and protective stance.

Soon, she took to helping him in his kitchen, where she did some cooking for him off and on.

With the increasing closeness, she began telling him about his appearance now and then in her dreams. Blue, red, yellow, and purple dreams! The dreams of dance, songs and marriage feasts! Of starry-nights, changing seasons, blossoming flowers, ripened fruits! Of the clouds, cloudbursts, flooded rivers, raging seas! Of the dense forests, chirping birds, fighting bulls, roaring lions! Of the deserted houses, formidable forts, high-rise temples, crowded railway platforms! Of the religious processions, milling crowds, village fairs and the wrestling bouts!

Then she took to visiting his house on Sunday as well, which was otherwise her weekly off. On these visits, she came dressed in the customary 'ghagra-choli-odhni', neat and clean, on her way back from weekly worship at the city's main temple, and passed some time, watching television or cooking for him. As her arrival usually coincided with his brunch, they often ate together before he settled down in the balcony for reading and writing, and she went about watching her favourite programmes on the television or cooking some easy-to-preserve dishes to last him for the coming week.

Her Sunday visits provided some company, besides saving him from the drudgery of the kitchen. The problem was her insistence to watch only South Indian programmes on the television, which he did not understand. However, she often held interesting chat sessions with him—even teaching him her language, which almost compensated for his time-loss on the television. Also sometimes, she confronted him with some problems facing her family or neighbours, which he could easily solve, earning her goodwill.

*   *   *

Chapter 4

He was a committed 'Nastik'; Atheist, Non-believer. He was very sure that on the basis of experience down the ages, the humankind has got divided into two schools of thought; 'Astik' (Theist) and 'Nastik' (Atheist). Further that Astiks, who believe in God (Believers) are in an over whelming majority the world over and Nastiks, who do not believe in God (Non-believers) are in a microscopic minority. While the Astik School of thought all over the planet earth has devised various religions consisting of a plethora of rituals, the Nastik School simply believes in materialism.

He was ever thankful to Gurbux Singh Preet Lari, Khushwant Singh, Mohinder Singh Walia, Darshan Singh Maini, Sasthi Brata, Vimla Patil, Yogesh Snehi, Prof. Yash Pal, Stephen Hawking, Nicolaus Copernicus, Galileo, Isaac Newton, Sigmund Freud and the likes, whose avid writings and works had shaped his perceptions about life, which he treated as universal truths. Likewise he ardently referred to the dailies/periodicals namely The Tribune, The Indian Express, Hindustan Times, Reader's Digest, India Today, Tarksheel, Preet Lari, Ajit Punjabi, Desh Sewak, Punjab Kesri, Amar Ujala, Dainik Bhasker etc. for sharpening his thought process with their multidimensional and balanced flow of knowledge. Also, he treated internet as the most dependable one stop source of knowledge. The work of 'Tarksheel Society Punjab (Regd.)' was his source of inspiration for self-confidence.

Being a Nastik, he did not recognize the existence of so called God, heaven, hell, soul, salvation, ghosts, 'jadoo-tona' and life before birth and after death, which he believed 'are only based on blind faith, and cannot be perceived'. All these, he felt 'are mere fabrications of the crafty priests of various religions aimed at self-aggrandizement, and patronized by the ruling classes known to assume the role of god-kings from time to time'.

As a materialist, he recognized only, the existence of Electrons, Protons and Neutrons, uniting to form Atoms of various types, which form four basic elements namely Earth, Water, Fire and Air; all having a free-for-all in the Space resulting in composition of the whole material world. Further that all bodies on the planet earth are the combination of these four basic elements in different proportions and the so-called soul is the quality of consciousness in each 'living body'. As such, there dose not exist any 'invisible, unchangeable and immortal soul' as claimed by the Astik school of thought. The consciousness of each living body, resulting from the combination of the four basic elements, exists with body and perishes with body itself, as it is associated solely with the body. Death occurs when the coordinated functioning of various body organs is interrupted due to old age, disease, injury, hunger, dehydration, suffocation, excessive heat or cold, fatigue etc. When a person dies, the wind in him stops circulating, the earth relapses to the earth, and the fluid to the water, while the heat ceases to exist for want of body structure. That puts an end to consciousness in the same manner as the sparkle vanishes from the lamp. Neither is there any other world, nor does the so-called soul fly away to the so-called hell or heaven, or to be born again. With this basic knowledge, he considered the so called reincarnation theory as meaningless and absurd.

He was in no doubt at all that a human being lives only once and after death there is no coming back in any living form. But his/her average seventy years of life are not without opportunities, disguised of course as obstacles. A beautiful woman/robust man who beckons him/her to seduce, an unpaved road that calls to trudge it, an offer of a career that beckons to choose it! What is required is only to shun ones cocoon of lethargy and comfort and take the coming obstacles head on, one by one, to live a zestful life.

He was no scientist, yet as do the scientists, he recognized the human body as a biological machine, which is a highly sophisticated and complex mechanism with unique functions and highly integrated structures. It consists of bioelectrical devices, and is self-producing, self-sustaining, self-adjusting, self-heating and fully automatic. For the proper maintenance of the body machine, the system exercises a shrewd control over the energy part of the mechanism, since it is this energy created by the metabolic process that keeps the body machine working. It keeps a definite portion of energy in the form of reserve, which it does not spend under normal circumstances. It exercises an expert control on the expendable portion of energy also. It also sees that the reserve energy remains intact and the expendable portion is always recouped. To ensure these conditions and to avoid all possible means of the dissipation of the energy, the system employs various protective devices like fatigue, giddiness, swoon, sleep etc. as required, and transports itself from the conscious (maximum activity) state to the unconscious (minimum activity) state. During these changeovers, which occur due to illness or under conditions of malnutrition or overwork, the non-vital organs, which are the main energy dissipaters in the system, are affected.

First the eyes, then the voice organ, next the ears, next the sense of touch, then the muscles and so on. In the condition of prostration, the entire available energy is directed only towards the maintenance of vital organs (elementary canal, heart, lungs, brain) and in fighting out the disease. In abnormal condition of a disease when there is minimum production of energy and maximum drain on the reserve energy, there is a gradual running down of the system. In case, in this fight, the system is at the point of the defeat with germs overpowering it, then as a last resort the system wages a desperate last-ditch battle with the energy. It either pours out the reserve energy in one single dose or fights a regulated pitched battle under the unconscious state (coma). If the system collapses and the vital organs fail to function one by one, the manifestation of activity stops in the body.

But, without doubt he felt that the human body is in a state perpetually developing for the better. He also felt that with the passage of time the man's prostrate gland will develop into two organs; one to control urine flow and the other as sexual intercourse facilitator. Likewise, the set of 32 human teeth will be replaced by two horseshoe-like structures to crush food, without the present day dental problems. Then, there will be no tissue as well, forming that tube-shaped sac called appendix attached without any use (other than the problematic appendicitis) to our large intestine. Also, he was aware of the scientists concentrating their efforts on the changes that take place within the cell during the aging process and trying to find out a suitable chemical that can delay the occurrence of these changes. With a few such chemicals already under trial, the most suitable chemical, if and when found, would be able to add more fruitful years to our life span.

The human brain, he felt, has immense capability, of which only up to about 13% has become usable so far. He also felt that the capacity of our brain under use can be sizably increased if it is used more often. Furthermore, he fully supported Prof. Yashpal (a renowned Indian scientist), in saying that 'the habit of accepting a lot of things on faith, without inquiry, can produce a mindset, in which many processing capabilities of the brain first go to sleep and then get eliminated. The brain grows through use, and the honest spirit of questioning rather than simply learning by rote is vital exercise for the brain'.

* * *

Chapter 5

His increasing closeness with Sapna blossomed within a short span. In fact, he never expected any favourable change to occur at first place, and if so, to occur so soon. But, the favourable change did occur and that too so soon.

It 'happened' during one of her Sunday visits to his house, when she prepared a dish and insisted upon feeding it to him with her own hand. But, before that, she threw many broad hints that day, which unfolded like a film reel.

By the time Sapna arrived, late by about an hour that Sunday, he was watching a Hollywood thriller on 'Star Movies' after finishing with the brunch, and leaving the main door unlatched in anticipation of her arrival.

She was in very high spirits, bedecked in brand new 'ghagra-choli-odhni', as if 'dressed to kill'. Her mustard-colour 'ghagra' (an ample skirt of ankle length) with magenta floral-design, sleeveless 'choli' (blouse) of plain magenta colour with plunging neckline, and plain mustard 'odhni' (a flowing cloth used by women in India to cover the head) with magenta frill, gave her the appearance of an Indian princess of yore.

To his utter surprise, for the first time that day, Sapna had applied make-up; complete with lipstick, nail polish, and threading of eyebrows. A double string of ivory-white beads adorned her neck. She had plaited her jet-black hair with a colourful 'Pranda' (a contraption of threads to plait the hair) into a Punjabi style 'Gut-Nagni', (a snake-like plait of hair) instead of the usual South Indian 'cascade' or 'hanging knot'. Her wrists were adorned with plenty of bangles. Rather than a mother of two, she wore the looks of an aspiring bride, returning from a visit to her parental home, following a short honeymoon.

Profusely smiling for the first time that day, she attributed her delayed arrival to her participation in the concluding function of a 3-day annual fair at the city's main temple.

Immediately on arrival, she slumped by his side on the sofa, for the first time, and almost snatched the 'Remote' from him, as if a matter of right, to click on the television, the South Indian channel of her liking. However, soon pretending failure, she nudged him to help her, with the 'Remote' still in her hand. Clueless about her intentions, he put on the channel of her choice and left the 'Remote' in her hand, where after pretending to watch attentively, she became motionless, as if unaware of the fact that with 'Remote' in hand, her forearm bedecked with bangles was resting on his thigh.

The telecast was showing a song sequence whereby the legendry South Indian hero was frolicking with the semi-clad damsel of his dreams in a valley of flowers. With her eyes glued to the television and giggling over the antics on view, Sapna that day was, for the first time sitting so close to him, he could smell her tantalizing body odour. So close, he could peep into the valley between her braless breasts under her 'choli' from above. So close, he could feel her breathing. So close, her ample 'ghagra' had almost covered his left leg. So close, provided the guts, he could have placed his left arm across her shoulders and kissed her cheek by lifting her face with his right hand under her chin.

But, with the sudden rush of the good things happening for the first time, his mind almost became numb. So, he could only think of the television changing over to an unintelligible language, and stood up to leave for the balcony, with the intention of reading his newspapers. However, when he was leaving, Sapna, with a smile close to blushing, tugged at his hand for the first time, and asked if he could prepare a cup of tea for her. Also, when she smiled, he chanced upon lovely dimples on her cheeks, for the first time.

Then, turning towards the kitchen as if obediently, he heard her authoritative order for the first time, "What about my brunch, including a heavy omelette too? I am feeling hungry as well".

Into the kitchen and making tea and omelette he thought, her actions could be her way of making the best use of what was available to her to live happily, as told by him.

The brunch served, he sat in the balcony to immerse in the Sunday Magazine sections of his favourite newspapers as usual. However, sitting there he realised soon that setting the television to play Hindi film songs in high pitch for the first time instead of the unintelligible South Indian songs of her liking, his Sunday visitor had become busy in the kitchen.

No doubt, he was pleased to find Sapna acting in the way she was. What he failed to comprehend being slow-witted was, all actions for the first time on her part that day were aimed at prompting him to have her in his arms. That she was to tell him, many years later.

With lowered eyes and a dish in hand, Sapna was standing in the bedroom, where she had called him from the balcony, on the pretext of fine-tuning the television. She had already put off her 'odhni' while working in the kitchen, and her heart was thumping loudly behind her tight 'choli', while a streak of perspiration taking off from her left collarbone region zigzagged into the valley between the domes of her breasts. She was breathing fast, resulting in rapid rise and fall of her belly button and its surroundings, above her 'ghagra', secured at the confluence of her pubic-pad and the desirable waist.

The emerging picture fired a hundred shots of libido and the debauchee sleeping inside him was fully awakened, to take benefit of the situation.

However, still posing to be no-nonsense-type, he lifted his hand to take hold of the dish.

But she refused to hand it over to him. Rather, she took a spoonful and proffered it towards his mouth.

Obeying like a child, he took the helping. Then, prompted by something from within for the first time, he gathered his wits and gave a helping to her as well, which she accepted as if she was waiting for it.

When they were munching tastefully, with the dish held by Sapna with both hands between them, gathering his wits again he placed his hands on her shoulders, followed by a gesture of head in praise of the preparation.

Seemingly, in acceptance of his move rather than expressing an adverse reaction whatsoever, she gave him another helping and accepted a similar treat from him.

Thus emboldened with her positive gestures one after the other, he moved his hands on to her bare waist between 'ghagra' and 'choli', and slowly pulled her.

On her part, she discarded the dish and clutched his shoulders, sending waves of sweet surprise down his nervous system, and in turn firing his sex mechanism into self-propelled action.

The consequence was a tight embrace, and in the heat of the moment, he kissed her in frenzy. While doing so, he felt something exploding inside him, in an automatic chain reaction, leading to orgasmic stimulus. The result was hasty ejaculation: an uncontrollable jet of the fluid, secreted by his seminal vesicles and the prostate gland, breaking from his semi-erect male organ.

* * *

Chapter 6

Well, according to Dr. R. Swaroop, the writer of 'You and your sex', 'there is nothing wrong in what is called the hasty or pre-mature ejaculation', which in his case had in fact exhibited the intensity of his desire to have Sapna for sensual reasons. As such, not perturbed at all by the hasty ejaculation, he continued fondling and kissing Sapna for a while, who reciprocated with fits of hugging and blushing. Soon his instincts came into form again and he felt the waves of passion knocking from within his loins. Thus with the renewed energy running through his veins and with fumbling fingers, he unbuttoned her sleeveless 'choli' from the back and undid the protruding knot of her 'ghagra' cord. However, in a swift move, she caught hold of the falling 'ghagra', and artfully extricated her shapely legs out of it, one by one. While she was doing so, he threw away his 'Rupa Frontline Banian' and became ready for the next action.

It took no special effort on his part to remove her unbuttoned 'choli' and once again, she clung to him; this time with her bare bosom pressed against his chest.

What a view it was in the dressing table mirror! A shining granite beauty in her stunning nakedness clinging to an athletic looking Punjabi! With stout domes of her breasts, a desirably narrow and supple waist, sturdy hillocks of hips and shapely thighs, she was all in all the bare-bottom 'Khajuraho-Yakshini' of his dreams, come alive to let him put into practice, the centuries old Indian art of lovemaking.

On to the bed, it was perfect act; pushing and pulling of a consenting woman by a desiring man, punctuated with huffing and puffing by both. How nicely Sidney Sheldon, that well-known prolific novelist, has described the act in a novel: ". . . . a mechanical construction of moving parts, fitting together into a coordinated functioning whole that excites!"

While the debauchee in him, riding cloud nine during the act, marvelled at the success of initiating a possibly prolonged sensual affair, Sapna appeared to be catching up for the loss of physical and emotional fulfilment suffered due to her husband's lack of passion resulting from excessive and compulsive drinking.

Demonstrating the total submission of a longing and grateful female to a protective and dominating male, she adopted some very thrilling and satisfying postures of copulation hitherto unknown to him. On his part, he repeatedly sent her into fits of ecstasy, by resorting to the 'Punjabi' posture, where by he 'did' by placing both her legs on his shoulders, followed by her, 'Going . . . going . . . gone!'

As it was the first union of two sex-starved bums with no interference at all, the 'session' with a number of 'active' and 'inactive' intervals went on and on!

It ended with a joint shower, followed by richly deserved coffee, prepared by Sapna, and heartily taken with heat-and-eat sausages retrieved from the refrigerator.

No doubt, the incident vividly registered in the depths of his mind forever and the amorous relationship established with Sapna that day, proved to be . . . . !

In its wake came the proverbial sense of achievement on the front of sensuality and much needed peace of mind in his day-to-day life.

In its wake came surprises adding distinction to his achievements in the art of seduction.

In its wake came many situations, which can best be described as dream-come-true.

In its wake came his triumph over some social taboos and egos, which facilitate exploitation of female of the human specie for selfish ends by the male in Indian society.

What he found in Sapna was, a woman of his liking whose faith in him was wilful and complete. She understood and fully implemented his philosophy of life to build blocks of happiness with whatever was available to her in the 'present mode'.

Sapna was attractive in real sense of the word! Her face and grace, her lips and hips, her eyes and thighs, all were in perfect shape and titillating in their own ways.

She was appealing! She was alluring! She was beautiful! She was cute! She was submissive! She was pretty! She was charming! She was docile! She was captivating! She was compliant! She was delighting! She was dazzling! She was desirable! She was elegant! She was exhilarating! She was endearing! She was enthralling! She was entrancing! She was electrifying! She was enchanting! She was exciting! She was fascinating! She was graceful! She was gratifying! She was glamorous! She was gorgeous! She was lovely! She was obedient and obliging! She was pleasing! She was pliable and polite! She was ravishing! She was smart! She was sweet! She was stimulating! She was stunning! She was supple! She was sexy! She was tempting! She was thrilling! All in one!

And that fitted very well into the outline of his role model for the game of love! How nice! Hurrah!

Sapna dreamed of him! She longed for him! She relentlessly showered her charms on him! She stood under the shower for long with the garland of her arms around his neck and her ample breasts rubbing against his broad athletic chest! She shared drinks with him sitting on his lap in the nude! The slit between her shapely thighs was always ready to receive his maleness! She spent countless hours in bed with him, willingly and happily reciprocating his advances! And above all, she loved him to the extent of madness despite many 'slips' on his part!

He could plan to have Sapna by his side any time of day and night! He could disrobe her! He could bend her! He could twist her! He could pinch her! He could bite her! He could mount her the way he liked!

On slightest indication, she went on her knees and elbows, to become 'ghorhi', (mare posture) so that he could mount her like a stallion!

Soon she sat pretty on his middle, like a yoga expert with parted thighs, providing the sheath of her nakedness to his sword of sensuality!

Still further changing places; she beckoned him to adopt 'Punjabi' posture by placing her legs on his shoulders!

He always found Sapna forthcoming and cooperative in the gestures aimed at intensifying the joy of their sexual union!

She loved making rhythmic whines to match the heaving and hugging on his part during copulation!

She expressed the joy of sexual climax with shrieks and shrills!

All such actions on her part gave him the sadist pleasure, coveted by men all over the world! Yes! Why not?

* * *

Chapter 7

No neighbour ever suspected any foul play on his part, as his image was that of a recluse, having no interest in the society other than his job. The atmosphere in his office was very cordial and the staff members never tried to peep into his private life. With no hindrance as such, Sapna all along kept his cauldron of sensuality from boiling over, by providing a steady outlet. For about one year or so in the beginning, their flights to the realm of sensual bliss took place almost every week, and the frequency later got reduced to almost twice a month.

With Sapna as the main breadwinner, no family member or her neighbour ever suspected her movements. The worry could be Parody only, who being under the spell of her elder sister was also manageable enough to be kept ignorant of their affair, or they so believed. The golden rule for him to keep Parody from suspecting anything black at the bottom was, to speak very little and very formally to Sapna in her presence.

His odyssey with Sapna generally took place around noon. Some nights were thrown in, especially during the winters. There was always no dearth of almost genuine looking excuses, for the long or short daytime ventures. For the rare night sessions however, the time-tested excuse was, for him to feign 'serious indisposition' and convey a 'request' invariably through Parody, to his ladylove to stay overnight at his house 'to look after' him.

All their ventures were well planned and Sapna always came on the dot, neatly dressed in the traditional 'ghagra-choli-odhni'. Though she was herself a good cook, yet to put the time on such occasions in proper use, she preferred fish, chicken, and other non-vegetarian preparations, ordered on phone. She was also fond of drinking, which she often confided in him was, mainly to make the indulgence carefree, and to heighten the ecstasy of copulation. Otherwise also, drinks were no taboo for women in her society, where homemade stuff was freely served 'as per custom' in marriages etc.

Immediately on pre-planned arrival, Sapna expected him to kiss and fondle her violently for a while in the lobby itself. In the process, her 'odhni' and 'choli' went off, exposing the upper part of her granite body with voluminous breasts, and igniting a thousand fires of passion inside him. In a few moments, she poured drinks; which they hurriedly gulped down their throats. Then they ventured into the bedroom carrying snacks and the second dose of drink. The first thing she often did in the bedroom was, to throw away her ample 'ghagra' and go in for a hot-and-cold shower, while he sat with his drink, watching television and anticipating the coming events.

Emerging from the bath with a towel covering her frontals, she made herself comfortable on the sofa by his side and lifted her glass.

With his obliging ladylove rubbing against him in the nude, he placed his arm across her shoulders and planted lustful kisses on her face between her sips at the drink. Pepped by the signals from her inviting body odour, the storm of sensuality began building up soon inside him. As a result, the blood supply rushed to the 'spongy kind of fibro-elastic tissue' denoting his maleness, consisting of 'a pair of corpora cavernosa and a single corpus spongiosum'; from the swollen part known as the bulb of the penis at the posterior to the greatly enlarged glans of the penis at the anterior'. That gave him a strong feeling of an upsurge, which became visible in the form of a tented arch of his 'lungi' over the crotch region. Sensing the development, Sapna rose with a jerk to stand in front of the dressing table, and taking the finishing sip at her drink, looked at her naked self admiringly in the mirror. Then she lifted her arms above her head and stretched her agile body, like a tigress getting ready for a hunt. Taking the gesture as an invitation for real action, he stood up discarding his 'lungi'. With his maleness aroused to its full glory, he took her in his embrace from backside, and made a few passionate picks with his teeth on the left and right sides of her neck. Fondling her breasts, he squeezed the nipples, thick with extra blood supply, indicating her flared up passion.

Acting in hurry and flurry, he found himself soon mounting his love partner, with her hips placed on a pillow at the centre of the double bed and her legs parted to the maximum; ready for an unrestrained give and take of sensual favours. The real action commenced, when he slowly pushed whole of his throbbing male shaft into the self-lubricated slot between her shapely thighs, to which she responded with sensual groaning.

The elevated location of his fourth-floor flat provided foolproof security against the noises being heard outside, and there was no need as such to speak in hushed tones during love play. So discarding all inhibitions, they were free to express their feelings of joy in words and actions. Consequently, the sexy shrieks and shrills of Sapna under his plough, mixed with his endearments as well as exchange of sweet nothings between them filled the bedroom, providing real thrill to the union of their bodies and minds. As the flight of amorous delight went on and on, the time seemed to stand still, giving them the feeling of being at the centre of the universe.

In the matters of actual performance, Sapna was an expert at many of the 84 postures of copulation, chronicled in the 'Kokshastra'. Once in place, she invariably fulfilled all his sensual aspirations; visual and physical, leaving no reason for any complaint. One of his obsessions was, to see her moving about in the nude, and she was fully aware of how to act. Hand in hand, they moved from one room to another without even a thread on their bodies. More often than not, they stood before the dressing table in an embrace for long. Her disposition usually left him wondering whether she was many-women-in-one! The whole affair was fulfilling and blissful enough, to keep the polygamous male-pig in him, from wandering away in search of pastures anew, but for some windfalls.

* * *

Chapter 8

He treated as valid only such 'evidence' or 'knowledge' to prove anything, that can be perceived through our five senses; hear, smell, touch, see and taste. He termed 'inference' and 'declaration' based on blind faith, recognized as means of 'evidence' or 'knowledge' by the Astiks, as full of flaws and hence not reliable. For that matter, he totally rejected the theory that some one called God had created the world. Rather he considered the material world to be the fortuitous combination of the four elements (Earth, Water, Fire and Air) which do not require a creator (God) to fashion them into design. 'Where from did come the Neutrons, Protons and Electrons uniting to form Atoms evolving into the material world, is still under research while the Astiks are also equally unsure of the origin of the world', he asserted.

As the most practical aspect of his belief, he did not recognize the traditional theory of liberation from pain. So long as the living body exists, it cannot be free from pain, because pain is an antecedent of life. Liberation from pain can be attained only on death. Anyhow minimization of pain and maximization of pleasure is possible. More over, pleasure should not be rejected because of its complicity with pain, and one should not reject the pleasure of this life upon the false notion of life beyond death.

Life wise, he was plain pleasure-seeking. He believed that pleasure is the highest need of life. Further that, so long as the human being lives, he should try for maximum enjoyment and keep the pain at its minimum possible level. In other words, people should live happily as long as they exist. But any action rendering more pain than pleasure to oneself or others is entirely unacceptable. Also, the real goal of human life is in the journey of life and not in its destination. To live a zestful and happy life, one should have a high goal and strive with a single-minded devotion to achieve the same. And the beauty of the goal is not in achieving it, but how one strives to achieve it. That is because 'some goals may not be fully achieved. Some jobs may not end in success. Some relationships may not be longer lasting. Some hopes may not be fulfilled. Some endeavors may not be completed. Some dreams may not be realized'. But falling short of one's goal, one should be proud of what one found along the way. One can always count on the wonderful things, which came into one's life because one tried to do something.

Money for him was the strongest thing on earth and the ultimate means of enjoyment. He fully supported Khushwant Singh that, 'the more money you have the stronger you are. You can buy all the wine you want and the most beautiful women will come running to you. With money, you can bribe witnesses to lie on oath and pervert the course of justice. With money, you can bribe judges, lawyers, politicians, preachers of religion, journalists and anyone else worth bribing to say whatever you want them to say'. But by all standards, money is to be earned by fair means. Unfair and filthy means should not to be used at all to earn money, because, these are detrimental to oneself and more so to the society. Also, the use of filthy means to earn money leads to selfishness, which in turn militates against social discipline and reduces the person concerned to the status of animals.

As amply and thankfully explained by learned columnists Vimla Patil & Yogesh Snehi, he believed as a 'universal truth' that man-woman relationship in the social groups world over actually stems from the 'subject-object' concept. Subject is the one who 'does' and the object is the one on whom it is 'done'. That comes from the sex act, which places the woman at the receiving end: With an active role for man as 'penetrator' and the passive role for the woman as 'penetrated'. That status of the woman has resulted in social attitudes, which have made her the object of verbally abusive terminology. It has in fact so 'sexualized' the woman, that the abuse may be targeting anyone, but it is the woman who is 'penetrated' and 'objectified' in the form of the victim's daughter, sister or mother. As such, the dilemma of woman is that she is in chains everywhere. In the same context, ironically the Indian society at its deepest core thinks that the man is born to rule and the woman to be ruled. Accordingly, the right or wrong actions of the man-dominated society have chalked out the life-graphs of women through ages in India. One may like it or not, women have all along been considered the 'property' of men. They have been kidnapped, punished, abandoned, left to live miserable lives as widows and even sold as slaves by all-powerful men. Things are not much different today. Women suffer the same humiliations even in modern India.

Therefore, playing the role subservient to the male chauvinistic pig, the Indian women have come to be divided into five types. That is as per their forbearance, bent of mind and other personality traits, as crystallized by the actions and reactions of the man-dominated societies through ages. The five types have their clear-cut role models in Indian mythology and culture and all the five of them stand out as true-to-life icons of their respective types. These role models known as 'Panchkanya' are; Sita, the wife of Rama; Mandodari, the wife of Ravna; Draupadi, the wife of five Pandava brothers; Ahilya, the wife of sage Gautama and Tara, the wife of the tyrant monkey-king Bali. All of them were legendry beauties and their luster caused kings, sages and others to covet some of them. The epics of Ramayana and Mahabharta describe the gigantic wars fought for two of them, Sita and Draupdi, whose beauty made Ravna and Duryodhana, lust after them. It appears that the life—graph of each of these legendry women is somehow replicated, like a jigsaw puzzle, in the lives of millions of Indian women even today. Suffice it to say, every Indian woman has a little or more of all the five types in her. As inheritors of the 'Panchkanya' concept through ages, Indian women are unique.

Fittingly enough, the Indian tradition links each of the five types of women to Earth, Water, Fire, Air and Space. Accordingly, the present day Indian women have great affinity to each elemental woman by the way they look, feel or react to the world around them. Most Indian women tolerate and accept the worst kind of injustice like Sita (Earth) and remain steadfast in their duty and devotion to their husbands and families. Like Mandodari (Water), they live a life of duality; with the turbulence of varied experiences on the surface, and a deep, silent core in their mind, where wisdom originates. They have an inherent gift of distinguishing between right and wrong. In a crisis, they know how to insist on doing what they consider right. Like Draupadi (Fire), they also hide storms of anguish, anger and revenge in their hearts. They believe that a virtuous, strong woman can ruin the most powerful of men.

Like Ahilya (Air), they have a dormant power buried deep down in their psyches. They have the strength to move like the air currents, and have the compassion to forgive wrongs done to them. Like Tara (Space), they seek a special luster of their own. They are intelligent, compassionate and large-hearted with vastness of space. From this niche, they spread their compassion and tenderness.

Feeling sorry for not remembering which learned columnist said it, he believed as a 'universal truth' that there are double standards in all aspects of life in India which one has to 'live and face' from birth to death. The tragedy is that these double standards are heavily weighed against the woman as compared to man. In childhood, all aberrations on the part of a son are dismissed as mere 'pranks of boys' while daughters are always taught, rather pressurized, to be gentle and suave or so to say lady-like. As a result, the women down the ages have been missing the joys of life in their pursuit to become gentle and suave. The matter does not end here. While a husband indulging in infidelity is always welcomed back into the family fold, a woman who dares to take the pleasurable path is considered beyond redemption. So strange are the ways of society that woman's subjugation appears to be a conspiracy of men and in this vicious circle the artificial conditioning is passed from mother to the daughter from generation to generation. Looking back one finds that the double standards of morality for men and women were prescribed by our religious texts and perpetuated by customs, conventions and traditions. For example, a man after the death of his wife was encouraged to remarry while a widow was not only not-allowed to remarry but was also expected, even forced, to commit 'sati'. While a wife had to be physically 'pure' for her husband, the men were allowed to keep any number of wives and concubines. It so happened that the women's bodies became the repositories of men's honour and men had an obligation to one another to hand over their women 'pure' while giving their daughters away through marriage.

* * *

Chapter 9

By the end of his second year in that South Indian state capital with the 'love affair' in full swing, Sapna sprang a surprise!

No! Not at all! It was certainly not her pregnancy! For that matter, she had already undergone tubectomy, and was thus incapable of conceiving. The 'surprise' was her distant relative Rachni, who stayed at his house for a month or so.

He had no intention at all, of keeping a young woman full-time in his house. But, everything happened so quickly; he had no choice, but to agree.

He found Rachni with a big suitcase at his door on a Thursday morning in early June, when he stepped out for a walk.

A day before that, Sapna had left along with her husband and the younger sister, for the native village of her husband. The emergency visit had to be undertaken following the demise of her ailing father-in-law, who had been recently shifted to his native village as per his wish.

Before her departure, Sapna had come to his house to get some money. It was also to inform him; she may not be back for a month or so, because, following the death of her father-in-law, some rituals were to be performed. Furthermore, as per pre-arrangement, her distant cousin Rachni was arriving in the city early next morning, for 31-day 'puja' (worship) at the famous 'Temple of Fertility', to seek blessings for a child. The 'puja' was scheduled to commence on the coming Saturday, the day of 'purnima' (full moon night).

"The coming guest was to stay at my house. But, due to the emergency at hand, there is no way out. So, I am entrusting the care of my visiting cousin to you". Sapna had said, adding that she was directing her neighbours to send the guest to his house on arrival. And she was off in a moment, much before he could react in any way.

"Hello Rachni!" he addressed the beautiful woman by name on first sight. She offered hand-folded 'Namaskar' in reply and the preliminary introduction was complete. Then, carrying her suitcase as a welcome gesture, he ushered her into the house.

To his question "When did you arrive in the city" she replied, "Just an hour back. The journey was very tough. I hope the 'devta' (deity) sitting in your city will certainly grant my wish! Yes or no? After all, I have come five hundred kilometres away from my home for the much acclaimed 31-day 'puja'."

Her Hindi was good but reply rather long, he felt. Anyhow, he opened one of the unused rooms of his house, which he had already prepared for her to stay. Then he took her along to show the kitchen, and of course, his spacious drawing-cum-bedroom with wall to wall carpeting, lavish curtains and the attached bathroom, before leaving for his morning walk.

Rachni was tall by all standards as compared to the average woman's height in that area. Comparing his own height with hers, he presumed her forehead would safely touch his nose in case she ever embraced him. Her complexion was wheat-like, and she looked more a Punjaban than a South Indian. She was smartly dressed in silken sari of aqua colour with a mini-blouse of the same stuff. Her face was egg-shaped with sharp features; pointed chin, long nose and gazelle-eyes; resting on a long delicate neck. Her slanting shoulders, graceful arms, ample breasts, narrow waist and corpulent hips, making her look like a model of Kangra paintings, conveyed the impression as if she was from some erstwhile ruling family. All in all she was a role model of the 'Padmini' type of woman described in the 'Kokshastra'. Aged about twenty-four years, she had an ample doze of vermilion in the parting of her hair and supported a big 'bindi' on her forehead: statement of a married Indian woman. Some how or the other, her over all manifestation appeared to him like a mango fruit; a fully ripe and sweet smelling mango, which had just fallen from the tree on to his lap.

It could be, he felt, she was educated enough to be made to understand that the childbearing capacity of a woman is based on her biological compatibility with her sexual mate, which cannot be altered by 'puja'. The only way to change it, he wished to tell her, was for her to have a biologically compatible mate and that too if she was herself medically fit to bear a child, which he hoped, she was.

Back from the morning walk after about an hour, he found his beautiful guest had already taken bath and changed into a sleeveless 'bhagwa chola' (saffron gown) of calf-length. She was then busy in her morning 'puja' at the makeshift temple, which she had established in her room, placing a small idol in a corner and lighting a brass lamp in front of it. She was carrying a brass bell in her hand and reciting something unintelligible in low tone, when she opened the main door for him. Then with the lowered eyes of a shy Indian wife, she went back to her room to continue the 'puja'.

In his attached bathroom, he found, his guest had used his medicinal soap and the hair removing lotion of Sapna. When he went to the lobby-cum-dining room in front of the kitchen after yet another hour and a half, Rachni was waiting at the dining table, ready with the breakfast of bread, omelette, and cheese, accompanied by chilly-sauce of his liking, and black coffee with sugar cubes placed separately.

"What would you charge for keeping me as a paying guest?" That was what Rachni said, when she spoke to him for the first time at the breakfast table.

"Nothing," he said getting hold of the breakfast plate proffered by her, and added, "I would be rather happy to see your wish for a child getting fulfilled!

"Why should you bear my expenditure? After all, I am nobody to you. Yes or no?" She fired the next salvo.

"Who told you that? Are we not related as human beings, the children of Adam and Eve, I mean to say?" He answered her single with a double.

"I gather you are from Punjab. I know, Punjabis are a loving people and broad-minded at that. Yes or no?" Rachni remarked halfway through the breakfast, perhaps in acceptance of the 'free' boarding and lodging offered by him.

"May be, your stay here would confirm your information." He flashed a ray of hope with an opportunity for her to try.

"In fact there could be some Punjabi blood in my veins as well. But that may be out of context here." She said after some time, posing to be a bit secretive, and in turn firing his curiosity.

However, changing the subject he remarked, "You have done a very good job of the breakfast. I wonder how you could locate various ingredients in my disorganised kitchen!"

"That's my realm man! After all I am an Indian wife." She replied with an air of pride.

"Mere wife? I presumed you were a teacher or something. By the way, what is your education?" His purpose was to bloat her ego to get her talking.

"Yes, a wife, and M.Sc. (Home Science) at that. For sure, I was a teacher before my marriage." Her reply was terse, but that served his purpose.

"So, I am almost to the point in my guess!" He remarked, with a sense of pride and looking into her eyes.

"More or less." She said, lowering her eyes and pouring coffee.

"Incidentally, does that give me the right to safely presume as well, you are more amenable to logic than the blind faith?" He asked, and putting two sugar cubes into the hot coffee, began stirring it with a spoon.

"May be, by and large." She said, and asked in the same breath, "But what makes you think so?"

"Why not? I just wanted to convince myself, my guest needs to be taken seriously." He said putting her off, and began sipping his coffee.

"My worry is to locate the 'Temple of Fertility', where I have to begin my 31-day 'puja' day after tomorrow." Rachni said later, as he got ready for his office.

"No problem! It is less than a kilometre from here on the main city road, to the east. You may visit the temple today or tomorrow to see for yourself, if you so desire. By the way, I take my lunch in the office and may return by evening only. You can cook something for you as you wish. Here, keep this duplicate key to lock the house in case you want to go out." He hoped he had made every thing clear to her, and left for his office.

*   *   *

Chapter 10

When he returned from his office in the evening, the guest was busy with the television in his room. That became obvious, when she offered 'Namaskar' with the 'remote' between her folded hands after opening the main door for him, and ran back.

Her hurry, he found soon was justified enough, because she was to catch up with the climax of the Dharmendra—Amitabh Bachan starrer, 'Sholey' on the small screen.

Watching intently, she stood motionless behind the sofa, while Sanjeev Kumar in his immortal role of a 'Thakur' with amputated arms and using merely his feet, mauled Gabbar Singh, the dacoit played by Amjad Khan.

As he changed over to casual wear unnoticed by Rachni and the armsless 'Thakur' was about to deliver the finishing blow with his foot, the police arrived to arrest the outlaw. That deprived the Indian cinewatchers for umpteenth time, of a chance to witness the 'killing of the dreaded dacoit' by the raging 'Thakur'.

However, while entering the bathroom for a shower, he had a glimpse of Rachni's face, glowing with a pleasant surprise. That was bound to be, because after depriving the audience of a 'great opportunity', the film director had cleverly arranged for the flame-buoyant Basanti, played by Hema

Malini, the heart-throb of millions, to sit in advance in the train compartment, which, with the mission completed, her chosen life-partner Veeru played by Dharmendra, boarded homewards, denoting end of the film.

As he emerged from the bath, Rachni joined him with two cups of coffee and a plateful of snacks, and told him, she had been watching Hindi movies on the cable for better part of the day, even skipping lunch.

So, she seemed to be hungry and rightly so attacked the snacks with gusto.

"Why? You should have had something earlier if you felt like." he remarked.

"No. I thought I should wait for the man of the house. Yes or no?" she said.

"How do you visualize performing the 31-day 'puja'?" he asked, provoking her to speak.

"It is like this," she explained, "I would be off to the temple every day, to attend the mass 'puja' from 10 am to 3 pm. There would be many like me, from far and away. All have to wear this 'bhagwa chola' day and night, symbolizing total submission to the 'God of Fertility'. There would be no under garments, unless one is through menses. The actual 'puja' will consist of correct chanting of some 'mantras', mostly in standing position as recited by the 'pujaris', like schoolboys' rhetoric. There will be short break for a frugal lunch provided by the temple authorities. There is however, no ban on whatever we eat or drink outside the temple. Also, the worshipers will have to observe 'maun' from sunrise to sun set all along, only exception being the recitation of 'mantras'. Furthermore, there would be no contact whatsoever with one's parents or in-laws, during 'puja' days. Each worshipper has already sent a sum of Rupees 11000/-, against proper admission slips issued by the temple management. Makeshift arrangements also exist at the temple premises for those who want to stay. But the general belief is one should not stay there, as far as possible".

Having heard the narrative, he was wondering over the futility of the whole exercise, when Rachni further told him, she had made long distance calls on his telephone to her parental and marital families to inform them of her 'safe arrival'. Also, that she had told them about 'free' boarding and lodging provided by him. She said her mother and father were in fact very happy to know about him. Her father had nostalgically spoken of Punjab from where one of his ancestors is known to have migrated to South India, under duress some generations back.

"How strange! We are so closely related and still you say you are nobody to me." he said, disrupting her narrative.

"No, no... I didn't mean that." She said, almost apologising for her morning remarks.

"Okay, tell me something about your ancestor who had migrated from Punjab, under duress some generations back." He asked, feeling genuine closeness with Rachni, and she narrated the following story, she claimed to have gathered from her parental family, which he felt could be true!

'Long, long ago, there lived a boy named Pala in a remote village Bhaura of 'Doaba' region of Punjab. Son of a well to do farmer, Pala grew into a tall and powerful man, and was recruited by the king of Jalandhar in his army. Serving the army, Pala mastered the art of fighting with dedication and rose in ranks in a short period. Once during a hunting expedition, Pala saved the king's life by killing an attacking tiger. Highly impressed with his act of bravery, the king appointed him as the commander of his palace security. That gave Pala an opportunity to see other members of raja's family including the beautiful princess who also took fancy to him. Soon the princess began to meet Pala in secrecy, but the king came to know through his intelligence department. As the king did not like his daughter to flirt with one of his servants, he transferred Pala away from the palace.

However, the love-bug compelled the lovers to become one, and one fine night they eloped to live as husband and wife at some faraway place out of that king's domains. The king sent his men in all directions to search for them, but in vain. Afraid of loosing his beloved, Pala took the princess to South India, and got employment with a king in that distant land. Living happily thereafter, Pala got two sons from his princess wife. With the passage of time, both his sons were also employed in the 'Raj-Durbar'. Every thing went on well for some generations, when India turned democratic in 1947 and the kings became commoners loosing all pomp and show. Likewise, those who lost employment with the abolition of feudalism, settled in various professions, and that was that.'

Coffee time over, Rachni went to her room for her evening 'puja' and later got busy in the kitchen.

* * *

Chapter 11

Rachni cooked a dinner of chicken curry and rice. At the dining table, he praised her art of cooking. She told him she was the eldest of four siblings: two sons and two daughters of her parents. Her parents-in-law also had two sons and two daughters, of whom her husband was the youngest. Her father was an architect of repute and her father-in-law a retired revenue officer. She had been married for the last four years and her husband was running a big general store. Both, her parental and the marital families were deeply religious with good social standing and were much worried over her 'failure' to conceive, she confided in him.

"So, you must be upset and very desperate to beget a child!"

"Yes of course, and so are my mother and father who are helplessly waiting for my likely fall from the grace!"

"Worried they must be! But, why your fall from the grace?"

"Do you know what may be in store for me, in case I don't beget a child within five years of my marriage? There would be a second marriage for my husband, relegating me to the status of an unpaid servant at my marital home or a life of contempt at the parental house. In fact, my marital family has already selected a girl for my husband and has sent me for this

31-day 'puja' at the 'Temple of Fertility' as the last try before making their intentions clear."

"What other measures have been taken . . . ?"

"Many! 'Yagnas' have been performed. We have visited a number of 'Tirthas' seeking blessings for a child. Donations are sent to the places of worship of various religions now and then and free food is served every Sunday to the poor and needy. All for a child!"

"That's alright. But what other measures have been taken? By the way, have you and your husband ever been medically checked up?"

"No. My husband is not prepared at all for a medical check up. My marital family simply says there is no need. They blame it on my fate. They say my husband's 'Janam Kundli' has the second marriage, written for him. However my father got me checked up secretly and the doctor declared me fully fit to conceive."

"Why can't you compel your husband also . . . ?"

"No! It is not possible! You know, it is a man's world. My husband doesn't want to get the stigma of being incapable of producing a child, by getting himself declared as such by the doctor".

"So, you have come here all the way to suffer the ordeal of this 31-day 'puja', and may be you are getting mentally prepared for the subsequent second-rate life in case of failure. In other words I may say, by proving to be a failure despite this 'puja', you are providing legitimacy to your marital family's designs to condemn you to the life of suffering. Am I wrong? How justified is your husband in sacrificing your life for his own whim? May be you are already reconciled to the possible suffering!"

"That is absolutely right! But, what can I do? God has created the woman to suffer only! If you think I can revolt, you are wrong. Nobody will come to my help. Not even my parents. Where do I go then? Same second-rate and contemptuous life! Our society is like that. God has made us so. I have full faith in God!"

"Believe me! I tell you! It is not like that! Man and woman are made of the same stuff. At the most, they can be described as complimentary and supplementary. Nothing more! That is all! There does not exist any God of the kind you have been made to believe, and for that matter, all the religious-minded people of the world! If there is any God, I tell you, he must be the one who 'helps those who help themselves'.

"What do you mean? Do you want to say, I will fail even after 31-day 'puja'?"

"May be yes, and may be no!"

"How both, yes and no?"

"Yes, it can be both. May be yes, and may be no".

"That is vague! I fail to understand!"

"What I mean, it can be both ways. Yes, you may fail. No, you may not. Yes, because there is difference between religious beliefs and the scientific knowledge. No child can be born to a couple not biologically fit and compatible. No, because it is still possible for you to bear a child, and live happily thereafter, in what you call a man's world. Some where in your education you must have heard something called 'survival of the fittest'. That is the underlying principle of life on this planet earth. The 'fitness' in this adage certainly includes the power to manoeuvre. 'Hunting with the hound and running with the hare' describes it more clearly. Its respectable name is diplomacy. You are medically fit no doubt! Now what is required on your part is manoeuvrability or so to say diplomacy. But, in your case, to be diplomatic you need to change your mindset. And to help you change your mindset, you need to strengthen your self-confidence."

"I don't fully comprehend what you say! Please tell me more. I am certainly desperate. For sure I do not want to fail!"

"The solution to your problem lies in your education. You said you are M.Sc. (Home Science). You must have read about something called elements. You know, we cannot change the nature of an element. But, we can certainly create some new products by mixing certain elements in certain quantities. In the same manner as water results from the reaction of two atoms of hydrogen with one of oxygen."

"Still I fail to understand what you say! Are all Punjabis so elusive?"

"May be so! But, having the Punjabi blood in your veins as well, you should at least be broad-minded enough to believe that I may not be wrong in what I have said so far."

"What do you want to convey after all?"

"Perhaps I can help you. That's all."

"Is it? Nevertheless, I wonder how! If that is that, I would love to . . ."

"Easier said than done. That is for what you need to have strong self-confidence baby! Believe me; I too want to help you in any case. Take my word. However, that does not mean you should abandon your 31-day 'puja'. Whatever I suggest doing, may fit in the whole scheme of things. No hurry!"

"What do you suggest after all?"

"Let me think." He said, and they retired to their rooms for the night, after Rachni put the kitchen in order.

The next day, Friday, was more or less eventless. Leaving home early morning due to an emergency in his office that day, he returned by dinnertime only. What transpired between them at the dinner table were only some words of praise from him for her art of cooking. She took the praise in right earnest and informed him of her inability to venture out during the day to see the 'Temple of Fertility'. The reason, she said, was her passion for Hindi films on the cable, one after the other, which were not allowed at her orthodox home.

*   *   *

Chapter 12

Rachni was up early on Saturday, the first day of her 31-day 'puja' commencing on 'Purnima', and by the time she gave him the bed tea, she was already through with her bath, and ready for the morning 'puja'. Her 'maun' began by the time he returned from his morning walk. After breakfast, she became anxious to leave for the 'Temple of Fertility'. No male was allowed to escort her to the temple, so he gave her a sketch of the road and explained salient features on the way, to reach safely on foot.

His office closed for the weekend, he was destined to stay put at home that day and the next. Had Sapna been in town, Saturday could have been spent in preparation and Sunday in sexual bliss with her. But, what to do in her absence?

Why to worry? The challenge was calling for him to face. 'Waves and Winds are always on the side of the brave,' they say. If these two 'W's can be won over by the brave, why not the third: Woman. But, the challenge facing him had the ingredients of all the three 'W's as well. Rachni, the Woman, had come like a Wave: unexpected. She was blowing in his house like Wind: a hurricane at that. Was she, as such, three times more difficult to win over? No, not at all! If her two ingredients, Wave and Wind, could be won over by the brave, so be the third: Woman. Why not?

Bravery was very much his cup of tea! Sure! Yes, for sure he knew all the tricks of the trade, the first being 'love begets love'. Now, what is love? So simple! Love, as per Collins Concise Dictionary is 'to have a great attachment to and affection for'. And 'to have passionate desire, longing and feelings for'.

Why not? That was all, what he had cultivated for Rachni, his newfound sweetheart, since her arrival a day before the previous day. Okay and agreed! But, where was the result? Not so simple as two and two becoming four. The target facing him and staring hard was a human mind and a rigid one at that. It was conditioned by social taboos and religious bigotry, genetically passed on, generation to generation, since the advent of the human society on the earth. He might be in a hurry, but some patience was certainly required to let the seed of his love germinate and grow sufficiently to bear fruit.

What should he have done as such? Wait? Yes! That was, what he was precisely doing that Saturday. Waiting for Rachni! Waiting, waiting, and waiting!

And hidden under the heavy folds of that wait, he discovered the pathway: serpentine and full of hurdles, leading to the mind of his sweetheart.

But, brave at heart that he was, he decided to plunge head on to make way, through the centuries old thorny bushes of customs, steep hills of conventions and deep gorges of traditions; like Sindbad the sailor, to reach his goal of making Rachni happy with the gift of a child, by acting as her biologically compatible mate. He had already ascertained, the woman was fit to bear a child, and in a tearing hurry at that. So, he thought it better to take up the journey sooner than later. 'Early bird catches the worm' and 'Where there is will, there is way', they say.

Waiting for Rachni, he visualised her arrival, on that sultry afternoon of June: exhausted from the first day of 'puja', mostly performed in standing position. That gave him an idea to help speedy germination of his love in her mind. So, following intuition, he boiled some almonds, dates, raisins and poppy seed in milk, passed the stuff through mixer, added some honey and placed a jug full of the drink so prepared in the refrigerator to cool.

Rachni was very much exhausted as visualised by him, when he opened the main door for her, on return from the 'puja' at the 'Temple of Fertility'. There were beads of perspiration on her forehead and her face was tense. She was so to say, completely down and out.

Without even exchanging a glance with him after offering the customary hand-folded 'Namaskar' in 'maun', she went straight to his airy-room, and slumped on the sofa: listless. Seeing her in that pitiable condition, he increased the fan speed and ran to the refrigerator. Returning with the jug full of nourishing drink along with a glass on a tray, he affectionately offered a glassful to her.

She expressed her approval with a gesture of hand after a couple of tasteful sips, looking quizzically at the drink and thankfully at him. Almost nibbling at the drink and relishing the crushed dry fruits, she took two glassfuls. Returning the empty glass to him, she shifted to the bed at his instance and fell flat, with a sense of relief on her face. Taking care not to touch her, he removed the pillow from underneath her head and instructed her to adopt 'shavasan' (corpse pose): placing her bare arms parallel to the body with palms downward, legs straight with feet slightly apart, toes falling outward, and head turned right with eyes closed. Then he asked her to take deep breathing: slowly inhaling and slowly exhaling.

After she was through with about twenty motions of deep breathing, he told her to breathe normal and relax. To relax, he directed her to concentrate on her toes and presume as if her feet had gone limp beyond control. Likewise, under his guidance, she systematically progressed to relax her calves, knees, thighs, hip-zone, stomach, chest, hands, forearms, shoulders, neck and head, and finally concentrating her stream of thought inside her forehead. Here, he directed her to recite in her mind without stopping, the mantra of self-improvement: I am the master of my fate, and I will live honourably!

After so serving Rachni, he went to the kitchen, prepared his cup of afternoon coffee, and took the same, sitting by the dining table. When he went to his room again, Rachni was fast asleep in 'shavasan'. She was fully relaxed and breathing slow. Her head was turned right, arms placed parallel to the body, legs straight and slightly apart with toes falling out. With the speedy fan giving the shape of her curvaceous body to the thin cloth of her 'bhagwa chola', all her contours were discernible in minute detail.

How strongly he wished to sit on the sofa, to gaze sensually at the sleeping beauty! How passionately he desired, to pass his hand over her; from bulky breasts down to pubic pad and further to the parting thighs, all seemingly crying for a biologically compatible mate, to impregnate their mistress! However, afraid of disturbing her, he tiptoed out of the room, closed the door securely, and got busy in reading Thomas Hardy's novel, 'Far from the madding crowds'.

* * *

Chapter 13

Reclining on the dining table with back to his room after sunset, he was thinking of the dinner, when he felt a gust of breathing on his ear and heard a female voice, "I am the master of my fate, and I will live honourably!"

It was Rachni, energetic and fresh after a sound sleep and bath! He could smell her tempting body odour mixed with the scent of Sapna's rose-spray. Almost perplexed at her closeness and fumbling for words, he extended his hands towards her face; with palms open. Obeying, she bent forward and brought her face between his hands, allowing him to caress her cheeks, and at his instance, sat on the nearest chair. Majestically!

Immediately, he got up, filled two glasses of pomegranate juice, and placed the tray in front of her. Offering one to him, she lifted the other glass for herself. After few sips she remarked, "Wonderful! What a hectic day it was! But for your care and affection, I would have abandoned the 'puja', and left for home by the first train, to die childless."

"Buck up! You are a courageous girl! A part Punjaban at that! By the way, what happened at the 'puja'?"

"There are many like me out there. May be, about five hundred of them all. There are also about twenty of those, who have come with their newly born, for a 10-day thanks-giving 'puja', but they need not stand. No way to speak to anyone due to 'maun'! Rest is all what I told you earlier. The whole affair is drab and tiring. Some 'mantras' even have to be recited while standing on one leg. Some of us may drop out mid-way, just out of exhaustion. That is what happens every year, I am told".

"But you will not be one of those who drop out! A brave girl you are . . . !"

"Certainly! But, I should be cooking the dinner now. Yes or no?"

"Yes of course, but, what about your evening 'puja'?"

"That can be skipped! What more is required now in the name of 'puja' after the daylong ordeal? Moreover, I am the master of my fate now, determined to live honourably! Yes or no?"

With this, Rachni entered the kitchen carrying the tray with empty glasses and called him for dinner later on. It was rice with mutton. Served with butter, beaten curd, and lots of salad. So simple, so nourishing, he could not resist the temptation of praising her.

Sitting across the table, between morsels of the tasty treat she asked, "How come, my failure to beget a child after 31-day 'puja' can be both yes and no? How yes and how no?"

"I am afraid; you may have to keep a heavy stone on your heart to comprehend that."

"Come what may, I am ready to face! Rest assured! I have full faith in whatever you say! Your 'mantra' of today afternoon has given me a lot of self-confidence. I was never so in the past. Besides, you are so caring. The drink you gave. What made you prepare it for me?"

"Let us go step by step. I anticipated you required the drink. I know you will require it every day. After all that exertion, I mean. Then the 'mantra'! I want you to practise it, day after day, forever. That is to help you become the master of your fate and live honourably by taking your own decisions. Of now, you have tested both of my remedies: the drink and the mantra. While the drink gives strength to the body, the mantra strengthens self-confidence. For that matter I may make it clear, you are only 4% body and 96% mind, and as per the subject of psychology, the mind certainly achieves, what it conceives and believes."

"Sure, sure! Must be so! I have certainly read it somewhere! But, what have you to say about yes and no? I am only anxious about the unsolved riddle!"

"Here you are! Inquisitive! But, for that you may have to wait, and till then concentrate on your 'puja'. That is because I don't want to thrust my way of thinking upon you." With this, he got up and retired to his room.

Next morning, Sunday, the second day of Rachni's 31-day 'puja', she left the home after breakfast without exchanging a word with him due to her 'moun'. The day was no doubt hot and humid as usual. Spending the day at home, he prepared the nourishing drink and placed it in the refrigerator to cool. He also visited the local market briefly, to replenish the kitchen.

Rachni came exhausted like the day before, went to his room straight, and slumped on the bed: sweating. Likewise, he served her the nourishing drink affectionately and instructed her, without touching, to adopt 'shavasan' correctly, relax her body, and repeat the given 'mantra' in her mind without stopping; with eyes closed. As anticipated, he found her fast asleep, fully relaxed and breathing slowly, when he returned to the room, after taking his afternoon coffee. This time, however, he sat on the sofa for some time, gazing at the sleeping beauty, and in imagination, fondling her sensual curves, to satisfy his libido.

Of his special attention was the bracket-like projection of her 'labia majora' enclosing the elliptical fissure known as 'pudendal cleft' in medical terms; located at the confluence of her shapely thighs below the pubic pad. It was discernible under the thin cloth of her 'bhagwa chola', shaped by the air pressure coming from the ceiling fan. However, with the determination of actually holding her soon under his plough, he tiptoed out of the room, and closed the door to sit at the dining table to read his novel.

Again, that day, Rachni came out of his room after sunset, fresh after a sound sleep and bath, and repeated his mantra in his ear, giving him a whiff of her breathing and the body odour, mixed with the pleasing scent of Sapna's rose-spray. Again, he poured juice in two glasses, which they sipped leisurely, discussing her day at the temple, without any additional information, after which she went to the kitchen to cook the dinner.

* * *

Chapter 14

The dinner was of his liking as in the past, and he gave due compliments to Rachni for the same. Some how he felt, she was lost in herself, as if making up her mind to say something difficult.

His hunch came out to be true after the dinner, when she ultimately opened her mouth to say, "You are doing a lot for me. I know. But, that is not all I want. May be I want more from you. May be as a part Punjaban, it is my right as well. Perhaps! Yes or no?"

"I don't follow exactly, what you say. I have already taught you the mantra of self-confidence. What more do you want me to do for you? I would love to . . . But I feel you are going strong with your 'puja.'"

"But you promised to tell me something about yes and no. Didn't you? I remember, you told me yesterday to wait and concentrate on my 'puja'. But I am desperate to know. I cannot wait any more!"

"Yes I did. But, do you still want to know that? Your 'puja' is going on well. Isn't it?"

"Yes, but I'm not satisfied! What if I fail, which I don't want to? At any cost . . . That is."

"What if you don't like what I tell you? What if you take an offence at what I have to say? I myself also don't want to fail."

"But then, you are teaching me to strengthen my self-confidence. What about your own self-confidence? Is your own self-confidence not strong enough to face the tangled web, in case I take an offence at what you tell me? Are you not very sure about the efficacy of your remedy for my problem, which you want to suggest by telling me how not to fail? I hope you too don't take an offence at what I have said!"

"So you are adamant."

"Yes, if you are adamant too! I don't care! I am certain; my self-confidence is gaining strength with every passing moment, to face the society. And for that I want your guidance!"

"Okay. Listen to me with a strong heart. With your strong self-confidence rather, which you say, is gaining strength with every passing moment."

"Please go ahead. I am dying to hear what you have for me!"

"That is good. I tell you now. You have been made to believe, you will be blessed with a child after 31-day 'puja'. That is not possible! Not possible at all! You are doubtlessly heading for failure! Yes!

The nature has created male and female in all living beings, including the humans, for procreation. That is to produce offspring, to carry forward the cycle of life. That I tell you is true even with plants. But let us only discuss the humans here.

As the medical science has made very clear by now, the ovaries of a woman produce one mature egg cell in every twenty-eight days of the menses cycle, which goes to the womb through the fallopian tube, with possible fertilization by the male sperm. The mature egg cell remains alive for about three days. In case, a sperm meets it following intercourse during these three days, well and good. It becomes fertilized to be nurtured by the womb, into a viable human offspring in nine months or so of pregnancy.

The three days or so, during which the mature egg cell remains alive to become fertilized, can be pin pointed easily. So, because during these days, the woman's body temperature increases by one degree centigrade without causing any side effects. In case the male sperm does not meet the waiting egg cell during these three days or so, the egg cell gets destroyed, to be replaced month after month of the menses cycle, until the woman is taken over by menopause in her late 40s.

Now what happens, other things remaining the same, some time the sexual mate of the woman is not capable of producing sperms, or so to say he is not biologically fit.

That, I am afraid, is the case with your husband. Were he biologically fit; he could have impregnated you by now, since you are very much fit, as per your claim.

So, you may take it for guaranteed from me, you cannot conceive unless . . ."

"Unless . . . what? I am impatient to know!"

"It is this 'unless', which is more important and needs to be heard with a strong self-confidence my brave girl!"

"Yes, yes, go ahead, tell me the 'unless' part of your riddle. I have understood everything else. Clearly!"

"Okay! Listen! You can't conceive unless . . . unless . . . you mate with a biologically fit man, other than your unfit husband."

"Is it? Really? But, that is very difficult. Rather impossible for a dedicated wife that I am!"

"Right you are! But, without this, the second rate and contemptuous life is hard staring in your face. It is one way or the other. Nothing more, nothing less! Life is like that! In case you want to suffer, nothing doing! If you want to live honourably, that is that. You are a brave girl! Nothing is impossible for the brave! The word 'impossible' occurs only in the dictionary of fools."

"You may be right! But . . . but . . . I am a faithful wife, I tell you!"

"No doubt! No doubt! I agree with you! But, how far that faithfulness is going to help you? What are you going to get out of it? By the way, does it in any way give a right to your husband, to play with your life? Should it not be reciprocal? Moreover, I tell you, the so called faithfulness of a wife you are talking about, is the result of double standards in all aspects of life among humans, which are heavily weighed against the woman as compared to man. In childhood, all aberrations on the part of sons are dismissed as mere 'pranks of boys' while daughters are always taught, rather pressurised, to be gentle and suave or so to say lady-like. As a result, the women down the ages have been missing the joys of life in their pursuit to become gentle and suave. The matter does not end here. While a husband indulging in 'infidelity' is always welcomed back into the family fold, a woman who dares to take the pleasurable path is considered beyond redemption. So strange are the ways of society in our country that woman's subjugation appears to be a conspiracy. But, the tragedy of this vicious circle is that the artificial conditioning is passed from mother to the daughter from generation to generation. Looking back one finds that the double standards of morality for men and women were prescribed by religious texts and perpetuated by customs, conventions and traditions. For example, a man after the death of his wife was encouraged to remarry, while a woman was expected, even forced, to commit 'Sati': death by jumping into the funeral pyre of her dead husband. While a wife had to be physically 'pure', the men were allowed to keep any number of wives and concubines."

"Too much and too complicated for me to cope with. I . . . I am not sure of what to do!"

"Don't get confused. Don't be in a hurry. You have the whole fifth year of your married life to decide and act. It is to choose between beating your marital family at its own game, and going down helplessly. It is nothing but plain manoeuvrability or what is respectfully called diplomacy. Think . . . ! Think . . . ! The decision has to be yours only! I have already given you the mantra! The mantra of success! To achieve what your mind conceives and believes!"

"How silly! You have exposed my precarious condition! I am standing between deep sea and the devil. Please tell me the way out. What should I do? Die childless or trudge the other path? It is not easy for me to decide! Not at all! Not at all! I have been fed on religious and social sanctions all along, attributing sinfulness or virtue to ones actions. I have been told to be true to my parental family, true to my husband and his family, true to other near and dear as per their status, and true to the society as a whole. I have been taught all along to maintain the sanctity of birth, sanctity of relationship, and sanctity of marriage at every cost. Here you are. Preaching the concept of biological compatibility of man and woman for procreation. Yours may be the practical approach to life, but I see immorality in it. What if your wife does what you are asking me to do?"

"Calm down! Calm down! My dear, calm down and think! That is what I advise. Do not act in haste. For the time being, you should forget what I have said. Let your strong self-confidence help you decide. Let your mind work on the problem and select the most suitable path".

"Okay! But I am desperate! I don't want to live the contemptuous life staring hard in my face. Under no circumstances do I want to allow the society to take me for a ride!"

"Think, think, and think my dear baby! Your argument may prove to be your stepping-stone. Does that mean you would like to consider the alternative? Anyhow, I don't press. After all you have nurtured the values of society for whole life."

"All right . . . ! I will ponder over the issue" she said, and stood up to retire for the night.

* * *

Chapter 15

Full five days passed in routine. During those five days, Rachni took to herself preparing the nourishing drink, and keeping it in the refrigerator to cool every morning. She also mastered the art of sleeping in 'shavasan' on return from the tiring 'puja'. As per routine, he returned from office and waited every day by the dining table, while she cooled herself for long in the bath after a sound sleep, to emerge from his room after sunset, fresh and energetic.

Only after five days on Friday evening, the change occurred! That Friday evening, Rachni was supposed to be in the bath, when he returned from the office sometime before sunset as usual. But, he did not have to open the two-way lock from outside with duplicate key to enter the house. Surprisingly enough that day, he found the main door ajar!

What he found on entry was more surprising! Yes, there was a big change!

Unlike other days, he found Rachni by the dining table, as if waiting for him, instead of cooling herself in the bath! Furthermore, instead of the usual 'bhagwa chola', she was wearing a sleeveless top of silver colour exposing her belly button, and a navy-blue silken 'grara'; both brand new. Her charming face had moderate makeup to the accompaniment of a multi-chain necklace, ear-rings, and a 'koka', all made of shining silver, matching with her top. Her head of hair was done up in a hanging-knot with a string of jasmine flowers. Navy blue bangles adoring her wrists and matching with her 'grara' gave her an enchanting look. Wearing high-heel sandals of Haryana-based 'Liberty Footwear Company', she gave him yet another surprise. That was, when she loudly uttered 'Namaskar' in welcome, instead of the usual folding of hands in 'moun'.

"Very good . . . Very good! But, what about your moun?" He asked in astonishment.

"Well, I am the master of my fate, and I will live honourably!" She 'declared' his mantra in reply.

"Here you are! So, you have begun to take your own decisions! Bravo!" He said, putting his hands on her bare upper arms, and shoved her on to the nearest chair.

Then, sitting over juice, he was just wondering at the unexpected change, when Rachni said as if casually, "Hm . . . it seems, I have some temperature today. Didn't you feel on my arms?"

"I don't know. Show me." He said, and moved the back of his hand on her bare upper arm: caressing. "May be, you are right. How come? Could it be due to exertion at the 'puja'?" He asked, with a worried look.

"Nope. Cannot be that. I left back during lunch-break today." She blurted, leaving him confused.

As he tried to wriggle out of the confusion, abruptly changing the subject she said, "Hm . . . but I am angry with you!"

"What happened?" He asked, still confused.

"I tell you. I cannot tolerate any more!" She further added to his confusion.

"What do you mean, after all?" He said, becoming serious.

"You are suffering due to me. That is."

"What makes you think so?"

"You are unnecessarily punishing yourself. May be due to my presence in the house."

"But I still fail to understand. Would you please elaborate?"

"Why? I find a partially consumed whisky bottle in the cupboard and two full bottles, besides a "Kajufenny". Why? You have never touched the bottle since my arrival. I know Punjabis love drinking. Why suffer for me? In our society as well, it is not banned. We offer liquor to gods too on certain occasions. It is also freely served at social gatherings. To celebrate, I mean. Even the women take!"

"Do you . . . ? And what about your 'puja'? I was afraid. Lest you mind it."

"No problem. I don't mind. Some time. It is good for health as well. In controlled quantity of course. It also emboldens one to speak out, what one cannot otherwise. That is."

"So?"

"So what?"

"So you approve?"

"Who? Me? Yes! But, oh my God! I am getting late for dinner. How silly!"

"Why bother? We will . . . Yes . . . Order the dinner on phone. Let us get going to celebrate now . . . !" He said with a pat on her shoulder, and led her to his room, where he made her sit on the sofa and put on the TELEVISION.

Taking the centre seat, she reclined; with half-closed eyes, her head placed on the sofa back and the legs carelessly parted. In that posture, her 'grara' and the top appeared to be exposing rather than concealing, her inviting thighs, and the voluptuous breasts.

In that posture of hers, he could very well read her mind speaking through body language.

The message was loud and clear for him: Come! O my chosen man! Come my compatible mate, I have decided to surrender my female charms to you. Come, I am yours now and forever. Come, I am hot today. Come, I am longing for your onslaught. Come, disrobe me, and hold me to your broad chest. Come, and explore my 'depth' with your 'height'. Come, plough my fertile land, and sow your seed. Come, and let your sperm fertilize my egg cell. Come, fulfil the vacuum within me. Come, give me a chip off your rugged block, and help me live honourably.

* * *

Chapter 16

Quickly, he had a shower and put on his night wear; 'lungi' with bare upper body, as they like in the South. Then he placed a 'Kajufenny' bottle, with two glasses, ice, soda, and snacks, on the table in front of his newfound love; then pretending to watch the TELEVISION.

Sitting by her right side, and ready to pour the drink, he asked, "How do you like? On the rocks?"

"Who . . . ? Me . . . ? Yes . . . No . . . As you will!"

May be her confusion was symbolic of her surrender he thought, and pouring the drinks along with soda and a couple of ice-cubes each into the glasses, he cordially invited her to join.

"Cheers!" he said, and "Cheers!" she repeated after him, like the 'mantras' she might be repeating after the temple priests.

"By the way, what are we celebrating?" Rachni asked after taking a double sip at the drink, and placing the glass on the table.

"Discovery!" He declared, following her suit in placing the glass on the table after two sips.

"Discovery? What discovery?"

"That . . . you . . . can . . . and that you have developed the confidence! To take your own decisions! Yes, why not?"

"Who . . . ? Me . . . ? Yes . . . ! But, what makes you think so?"

"May be . . . I can tell you only if you . . ."

"What do you mean?"

"Not so serious. It is only if you take two sips from my glass. That is."

"Not a big thing . . ." She said, and took two sips from his glass.

"That's my answer my dear. And that certainly makes me proud of you. Yes or no?" He said taking two sips from her glass.

Beginning the celebration thus, and taking two rounds of the drink in half an hour or so, Rachni became bold enough; to tell him she was a dancer of sorts in her college days. Then prompted by him during the third round, she stood up to dance, to the tunes of the television music.

It was first the dance of Helen and then Vijayanthimala, followed by Hema Malini on the television, which she duplicated in flesh and blood, giving a fascinating show of her charms and dancing skills. A number of times, giving her a standing ovation, he patted her back and held her by the waist, without any adverse reaction from her.

In a nutshell, it was all 'Dum dum deega deega . . . '(an old Hindi film song) for him!

They finished the dinner ordered on phone, with more Kajufenny, by which time the din of the city outside had also subsided.

Nibbling the sweet dish after clearing the dinner things, and sitting by her side to watch television, he asked Rachni, "How do you like your stay with me?"

"Wonderful!" She replied.

Encouraged with her reply, he placed his left arm across her shoulders along the sofa-back, and asked, "But you have not told me!"

"What have I not told you?"

"The decision . . . I mean . . . You . . ."

"The decision . . . ? You mean . . . I . . . ?"

"I mean . . . Yes or no."

"Yes . . . Both . . . ! Yes and no! I mean . . . !"

"How both yes and no? Do you disapprove?"

"No! Actually both! Yes and no, I mean!"

"What yes . . . and what no?" He asked, clutching her shoulder and pulling her closer.

"Yes for yes . . . and no for no . . . ." She said, without resisting his move and putting the sweet dish away.

"I don't get you. May be, you are turning out to be elusive". He said, placing his right palm on her left cheek.

"Yes for yes I simply tell you . . . Yes for beating them at their own game, I mean! And no for no, I tell you . . . No to remaining childless I mean". She said, slightly bending towards him.

"You . . . ? My brave girl . . . !" He muttered, and took his face closer to hers.

"Brave . . . ? Me . . . ? Yes . . . ! I am the master of my fate and I will live honourably! You taught me so. Yes or no?"

"Yes . . . ! But your temperature is still the same". He said, making an excuse to continue caressing her cheek with his right hand.

"But . . . You told me that day . . . It could be . . . Yes or no? I still remember very much . . ."

"O . . . my . . . ! Without any side effects . . . ?"

"May be . . . I . . . Yes!"

"Could be so!" He wondered, and kissed her right cheek for the first time.

"Yes . . . Me . . . I remember everything . . . You told me . . . No childless . . . Me . . . ! Yes or no?"

"How brave of you!" He uttered, and kissed her right cheek once more.

"How me . . . ? You naughty . . . ! Don't talk . . . !" She said, and almost fell on to him.

* * *

Chapter 17

Triumphantly, he fondled her thigh and beckoned her to rise after a few moments. On to their feet, he held her to his chest in front of the dressing table.

Embracing he found, her forehead measured exactly up to his nose.

Almost feverishly, he took off her top exposing the voluptuous breasts for the first time, and put her on the bed: sprawling. Then he removed her 'grara' to find she had no underwear, and threw away his 'lungi'. Standing thus for a precious moment by the bedside, he viewed himself as the legendry 'Maharaja', described by Dewan Germany Dass, appearing before his subjects with his throbbing male organ, as the personification of God Shiva.

"My God! How big!" Rachni exclaimed looking at his member in full form, and placed her hands on the parting point of her thighs, covering the love-pot in her whole nakedness.

In a moment, he bent over to her and fondling her breasts, twitched the sensual nipples, thick with flared-up passion. Then pushing her hands away, he pressed his right folded knee between her thighs, exposing his target, hiding smug!

With a kiss on her forehead, he took position between her parted legs, and with his right hand, introduced the head of his member into her vaginal cavity, lubricated with excitement.

Clutching his shoulders with both hands, Rachni encircled his lower thighs with her legs, in a way permitting him to go ahead.

Then keeping his body weight on his elbows with forearms under her shoulders, he affectionately held her head in both hands: ready for the action!

"Oh my . . . ! Here you are! What a forceful thrust! Seems to be from a different world! I have never experienced such an ecstasy!" She exclaimed, when he pushed his maleness into her female cavity with a few caring hip-jerks, and united his pubic pad with hers, uttering sweet nothings.

Entry complete, he took her in a tight embrace, pressing her breasts against his chest.

As he kissed her forehead in that posture, Rachni clung to him with full force muttering endearments. But, full of passion as he was for the past many days visualising Rachni under his plough, he could not hold himself any longer, and a jet of dense liquid issued from his within into her 'depth', which she received with closed eyes and inward straining of her legs.

The circle complete, his member became flaccid, but he continued cuddling and kissing his partner in the same position, to which she also responded without hesitation. With the two lovebirds eager to fly through the sky of sexual bliss, the things looked up soon and his member again came into form inside Rachni's depth, whose passion was already flared up.

Then his hips began to rise and fall in a slow concerted manner, with occasional halts for minor adjustments of the posture.

The intercourse continued fairly long in fits and starts, and thrice he felt the sudden convulsions of Rachni's vaginal muscles gripping his maleness, accompanied by her inward straining of legs. Well, that was the repeated climax of her sexual fulfilment resulting from her complete surrender. As she was about to repeat her inner action for the fourth time, he felt something ready to gush out from his within.

Uncontrollable during those moments, his up-down motion suddenly became speedy and the dense liquid flowed once again, into the depths of Rachni's curvaceous body. Her fourth-time vaginal convulsions also erupted by then, and both of them held each other with full force, becoming a single entity.

The hurricane of libido over with the climax, their grunting and vibrating bodies fell motionless; feeling the coveted bliss, and mindless about the world outside.

Fully satisfied, they separated after some time and made a show of sleep: clinging.

However, the sleep evaded them and soon they took to caressing each other and muttering endearments.

"Did you like it?"

"Wow! How big! At the first look, I thought it might give pain. Nevertheless, I know you are so caring! When it came, I really felt we are made for each other. Yes or no?"

"Happens! You are so exciting! How I desired all these days! Never knew, you will . . . !"

"But, I decided in your favour last Sunday night itself, after you explained the reality to me. Only I could not dare due to shyness all these days. That was despite making up my mind a number of times to barge into your room around midnight, under the pretext of sleepwalking or something! Really!

"Is that so?"

"Anyhow, you . . . naughty . . . ! You enticed me with love and care . . . to fall for you. Now I am yours! Forever . . . I mean. Yes or no?"

"No doubt at all in what you say. I agree. But your hints became clear today only. And I simply followed those hints to reach my destination."

"What were those hints? I would like to know?"

"First of all, your 'bhagwa chola' and day-time 'maun' were gone. Then, your hint of temperature without any side effects. In fact I tell you, the message was so loud and clear, that at one point I just had the mind to lift you bodily from the lobby straight to the bed."

"Right you are. But I was in a hurry, and so the broad hints. You know, I have already wasted almost a week. What if the precious three days of high temperature were also lost? A colossal waste of your effort at motivating me, and the loss of once-in-a-life-time opportunity, followed by a life of repentance for me! That is because I cannot stay with you beyond the 31-day 'puja', to wait for the maturing of the next egg cell. Yes or no?"

"Very smart of you honey! But then you could have found some one else back home. Yes or no?"

"Easier said than done! Do you feel I could have found a man of my choice back home without the episode eventually becoming public? Moreover, where could have I found a Punjabi, biologically fit for the part 'Punjaban', that I am?"

"Very far-sighted of you! Really!"

"Above all, I feel I am only made for you. Yes or no?"

"Okay I agree. By the way, how many postures of lovemaking do you know? Do you know, 'On-all-the-fours', and 'Punjabi'?"

"No . . . I am shy of discussing that . . . I mean . . . I am your obedient . . . I will do only as you want me to . . . I have already told you, I am only made for you. Yes or no?"

"What about 'Woman-atop-the-man'?"

"How I say? I have told you, I am shy of . . . I will only obey. That is. I mean."

And with such lustful exchanges going on and on, libido hovered around for whole night, making them to undertake one more long session of lovemaking.

So it was really roses-roses all the way for him, with Rachni fully cooperating in his sexual . . . err . . . sensual fantasies; 'Woman-atop-the-man', 'On-all-the-fours', and of course the 'Punjabi'.

* * *

Chapter 18

When he woke up by the late forenoon, he found Rachni sitting on the sofa, in a brand new 'sari' of pink colour, and gazing at him with a tranquil look on her face!

"What happened? What about your 'puja'?" He asked.

"No. I did not go. Now that I have taken the logical path, the 'puja' has no place in my scheme of things. By the way, brunch is ready, and I am feeling hungry." She said in one go, as if suggesting he should immediately go in for the much-delayed morning ablutions.

After the brunch, Rachni turned down his suggestion to bed with him.

"No, I have to visit the local market." She gave the terse argument.

"Everything is available in the house. Why visit the market?" He asked in surprise.

"Yes, I have to . . . There are certain formalities. Besides, I am throwing a party today evening." She said, and went out, closing the door for him to sleep.

Having slept for better part of the day, he was reclining on the sofa in 'lungi' after a bath in the evening, when Rachni appearedinhisroombedeckedinPunjabibridaldress: Sparkling red and heavily embroidered 'salwar-kameez-dupatta'.

With her face in 'ghungat', she placed a loaded tray and two garlands, on the table in front of him. Then, peeping through the 'ghungat', she put a garland around his neck, applied 'tilak' on his forehead, waved a flaming brass lamp, with lowered eyes, seven times in front of his face, offered a sweetmeat to eat, touched his feet reverently and sat on a stool facing him.

Taking a cue he reciprocated, by putting the second garland around her neck, lifting her 'ghungat', applying vermilion mark in the parting of her hair, offering a sweetmeat, and kissing her done up cheeks.

Then, they lifted the glasses of pomegranate juice, and giving a sip to each other, finished the drink in slow gulps.

The formalities over, Rachni stood up with folded hands and wished him, "A very happy wedding!"

He took her in a tight embrace with "Same to you" and gave her a hundred-rupee note with a kiss on her lips as 'shagun'. Thereafter lifting the tray, she left the room, as dramatically as she had come.

Soon, Rachni returned with another tray, this time stark naked, but for an apology of an underwear fashioned out of fresh 'paan' leaves and roses. Also, she was still wearing the 'wedding garland'.

As she sat again on the stool placing the tray on the table, he asked why did she not sit on the sofa by his side.

"No, I would like to serve my husband sitting in front of him. In the true Indian tradition. Yes or no?" She said with folded hands and lowered eyes.

To his question, "Why have you discarded the bridal dress?" She replied, "Marriage ceremony is over. This is party time for the two of us in the tribal way. And I understand my chosen mate loves to gaze at me in the nude. Yes or no?"

"Me? . . . You? . . . Who said?"

"Yes . . . yes . . . ! As your better half, I should know your thoughts as well . . . ! Yes or no?"

"What about you?" He asked, when she poured 'Big Boss' Kajufenny on the rocks, and offered the drink to him.

"No . . . ! It is only for my hubby to decide, whether he likes to share his drink with me in the party". She said.

Astonished, he just uttered, "Happy wedding" and taking a double sip, put the glass to her lips.

It was then a rare 'party' of the 'newlyweds'; sharing drinks and affections, during which Rachni gave fascinating dance performances. What a view she was, dancing in her nakedness!

The dinner for two ordered on phone at the instance of Rachni, arrived at the appointed time, and they enjoyed it in an out-of-the-world situation.

Then taking a mini walk within the house, hand in hand after the dinner, they made it to the bed, and plunged head on into the sea of sexual ecstasy under the relaxing red light. Suffice it to say that leaves and roses used to fashion 'the apology of an underwear', which Rachni had come wearing to the party, were scattered on the carpet. Also lying in a heap on the centre table were the two 'wedding garlands'.

While the two male—female figures on the bed intermingled in an effort at giving and taking sensual delight, submissive shrieks and moans of Rachni filled the bedroom, which of course none other than the two of them heard from that 4th floor flat. The nakedness was on full show without hesitation; stout breasts, corpulent hips, shapely thighs and highly flexible waist of the heaving and whining female, gladly coping with the male's onslaught, hidden from the world outside.

"Why this marriage thing?" He asked Rachni, with an amorous nibble at her sensual nipple, sometime after they recovered from the first round of lovemaking.

"No marriage thing . . . ! It is marriage pure and simple! No disgrace to the holy ritual on the 'suhagraat' please!"

"Okay! Why this marriage?"

"Yes, it was necessary. I do not want to carry a bastard. Yes or no?"

"But, both of us already have legally wedded spouses!"

"But a man can always have more then one wife in the orthodox society of India! And so in many other parts of the world including Africa and the Islamic countries."

"How come, you believe this?"

"Don't you know our history and culture? What about various God-kings and emperors of yore with many a wife each, whose lives are considered exemplary even today? Should I name a few of them for you to remember?"

"But, I am not a king! I am a lesser mortal! Yes or no?"

"But for procreation, that doesn't matter! The difference between king and the pauper only lies in the crown of the king and rags of the pauper. Nature of the body and mind is the same in all human beings. The human is human. No difference at all. Yes or no?"

"Yes once more. Then, what about you? How do you justify a woman having two husbands?"

"Here is my point my man. You are no naive. Why do you forget that legendry wife of five Pandav brothers, some of whom had other wives as well? For me, it is only the question of two husbands. And what about polyandry still prevalent in some tribes in our vast and unwieldy country, despite the modern laws to the contrary? Yes or no?"

"Very ingenious of you!"

"I follow your line my lord! But, I have wasted a whole week. Yes or no?"

"No. That was necessary to consider all aspects of the problem. But, you are intelligent enough to decide by the onset of the precious three days, which are the key to pregnancy. Furthermore, you were also bold enough to tell me of the key period, by casually referring to your body temperature. I am really proud of you!"

"Very many thanks! But, may I now press your legs, as an obedient wife will, in India?"

"Yes, you can, if you wish. But, no compulsion. I treat husband and wife as equals."

"But you said they are complimentary and supplementary." She reminded, and took to pressing his legs, in the nude.

After the night of lovemaking, they spent better part of the next day in sleep, and were ready again by the evening for a night of fulfilment. An additional activity, they added to their routine that day was, taking of joint showers in the attached bath, making the water, a witness to the union of their bodies and minds.

The 'honeymoon at home' lasted until the end of Rachni's supposed 31-day 'puja' at the 'Temple of Fertility', for which he got some leave as well from the office. Though the frequency of sexual bouts later got considerably reduced with an occasional daytime indulgence, yet they tried to live as close to Mother Nature as possible those days, by remaining in the nude most of the time.

As the time goes on without stopping, the day of departure came, and Rachni was off by train. She was frantically waving her hanky until she vanished from his view, leaving him starry-eyed at the railway station.

Her telephone call came through after about a month of her departure. Bubbling, she told him she was 'carrying', and her marital family had since performed a 'yagna', while her husband had thrown a party to his selected friends at what they described as the 'success' of her 'puja'.

In due course, she gave him another call. "Congratulations!" She bubbled again, and informed him of a son born to her. About two months thereafter, she arrived with prior intimation, to live with him, in the name of '10-day thanks-giving puja' at the 'Temple of Fertility'.

He was all agog, when on arrival at the railway station, Rachni handed the male-child over to him remarking, "Your son is very naughty like you," and touched his feet, as an Indian wife will, on meeting her husband.

"No surprise! After all he is a 'Punjabi-Puttra'!" He exclaimed, and hugged them both.

"So, becoming the master of your fate, you have beaten them at their own game!" He almost sang into her ear, still clutching.

"And I am living honourably as well! Yes or no?" She added.

* * *

Chapter 19

During the first year of his stay in that house, he saw very little of Parody, who was then a primary school student. Her real name was given out to be something resembling the name of a South Indian hill. But he could never ever remember that long-long name. Her domestic name was 'Munni', but he preferred calling her 'Kanya', while the name Parody only existed in his mind.

He saw Parody slightly more in the second year of his stay, when she joined high school and prompted by her elder sister, occasionally came to his house to ask for solutions of her educational problems, or so to say for 'home work' given by the teachers.

Originally having a frail physical constitution, Parody began picking up in health and height after first menstruation at thirteen. Her first menstruation was greeted by confining her to a room for nine days. That was followed with a community feast on the tenth day, as per custom; to announce that having entered puberty, the 'girl' had become eligible of becoming a 'wife'.

Becoming a wife at thirteen? Child marriage? Well, there is nothing to get alarmed! This (child marriage) is happening in many a community in India despite law of the land providing otherwise. Yes! That is the wont of real India; existing behind the facade of democracy, social justice, equality before law, and many more similar epithets resulting from the gimmickry of political self-seekers, data-flaunting bureaucrats, religious sycophants, and social touch-me-nots.

When Parody came to his house to seek his 'blessings' after the community feast, he bestowed on her, the right to have an egg and a glass of milk, on daily basis from his kitchen as long as she wished. This was to take care of her mal-nutrition; in a subtle move recognizing the 'secret services' rendered by her elder sister, to keep his libido under control.

Her entry to the puberty stage making her socially eligible of becoming a wife, gave Parody a sense of responsibility. This in turn made her conscious of grooming herself. With this, she began helping her elder sister in door-to-door domestic jobs as well.

A teenaged girl working on domestic jobs? Yes, child labour is another slur on the face of Indian democracy! We have laws to curb it, but the implementation part is tardy beyond redemption.

Parody's visits to his house became a regular morning feature, when she came to polish off the daily supply of egg and milk, which was soon converted into wholesome breakfast by adding a stuffed 'prantha' or alternately bread and butter to it.

Her daily visit continued almost uninterrupted throughout his stay in that city of 'joy'. All along, it gave much needed nutritious support to her. Besides, her daily visit served as his dependable communication link, with the family of his partner-in-adultery. Yes, adultery also continues in India despite laws prohibiting it. Why India alone? Is adultery not found in the human societies all over the world, next to prostitution? Leaving aside those few who have failed somehow, can a man worth his salt anywhere say on oath that he has not bedded or aspired/tried to bed a woman other than his wife?

May be Parody came alone or with her elder sister, one thing soon became certain that like her elder sister, she too felt psychologically comfortable and secure in his house, though for different reasons. While the 'comfort' of Sapna stemmed from her satisfying affair with him, for Parody, it came from his over all protective stance.

As the two sisters moved in and out of his house day in and day out, he continued making conscious and unconscious efforts to keep them in good humour; again for different reasons. To the elder as 'lover' and to the younger as 'cover'. So much so, he did not mind even if sometime they took home some cooked or uncooked vegetables or other eatables from his kitchen. He also maintained a steady stock of cold drinks of their liking.

As a helping hand, Parody would without hesitation also run to the local market, to fetch milk etc. for his kitchen, whenever required. He generally allowed her to keep for herself, the small amounts of money, which she brought back from the market as leftovers from the small purchases.

By the time Parody joined standard IX in high school, she became responsible enough to take up part-time jobs in some houses independently, where she worked before and after school hours. The idea was to augment the family income. On certain days, she also came to his house, to work in place of her elder sister, in addition to the routine morning visit for the wholesome breakfast. Though he generally maintained a studied silence in her presence as a precaution against exposure of his affair with her elder sister, yet Parody respected him as a mature adviser, and always had a stream of questions to ask. Due to her ever-increasing confidence in him, even films and love affairs of some girls of her locality sometimes found mention in her talks with him.

Occasionally, Parody accompanied him to the central city market, to make domestic purchases. On the way, she sat with him in the local bus or three-wheeler, unintentionally rubbing her stout body against him. Her 'favourite' during these visits was 'Quality Ice Cream' at the market square, which they always enjoyed after shopping.

Another thing about Parody; besides being under the emotional spell of her elder sister, she was very much religious minded, and always decided on the good or bad of her actions on the basis of religious sermons. Whenever she visited any place of worship, she invariably brought 'prasadam' for him, which she said, was for his health and happiness. Despite knowing that he was a non-believer, she claimed to be doing this for her own belief in God, who she said, was "always watching our actions; good or bad, to decide to send us to heaven or hell after death". He tried to convince her that in order to keep the lesser mortals under subjugation, some clever people had conceived the so-called God, with various names and forms as known to the humans. He also tried to convince her about futility of humans' belief in so-called fate, but all such ideas were Greek to her.

On the education front, Parody was way ahead of her years. By the time she joined standard X, her Hindi and English became reasonably appreciable. Her memory was unbelievably sharp and so was her power of argument. She was very quick-witted and inquisitive as compared to other girls of her age. She was also member of the school's dance and dramatic group, and had many prizes to her credit. A number of times she invited him to watch her dancing skills in school functions, but, somehow or the other he always failed to make it convenient.

* * *

Chapter 20

About love and sex, he agreed with what the London based Pakistani Psychotherapist, Mrs. Shahrukh Hussain has to say (as thankfully quoted by Reader's Digest) in 'The Virago Book Of Erotic Myths And Legends': 'Love is as essential to us as breathing and sexual fulfillment as vital to our sustenance and well-being as food. Yet a taboo came into being at some stage, unannounced and unexplained, which reduced this indispensable and intense energy to a vice'. Suffice it to say that sexual intercourse is actually a great stress reliever and a booster of emotional and physical energy. The hard fact is that sexual intimacy between consenting adults improves health by promoting necessary neurochemicals and hormones.

Anger, he learnt rather late, is one of the major risk factors for heart attack and paralytic stroke, because negative emotions cause narrowing of arteries supplying blood to heart and brain in the long run. According to some eminent cardiologists including Dr. K. K. Aggarwal, of Heart Care Foundation of India, 'angry thoughts and the resultant negative emotions circulate and react with every cell in the body instructing the body to constrict the arteries, increase the pulse rate, and raise blood pressure. Repeated episodes of anger can lead to severe problems like heart attack and paralysis and sometimes even sudden death. Negative emotions like anger act as a slow poison, which kills the individual over a period. We should realize that during anger one loses the power of discrimination, so it has to be controlled much before it becomes full blown. The initial stage of the malaise is irritability and, therefore, its onset should be controlled at the earliest. It is also dangerous to run at a high speed while in a rage, as it alarms the whole nervous system, and chemicals such as adrenaline are released in large amounts in the body. Many exercises to control anger like observing silence for 20 to 30 minutes a day, speaking sweet and soft words and with every bout taking a walk or drinking cold water, doing 'Pranayam' are suggested'.

He was in the long run given to understand that in order to carry out a given task one needs proper mood, inspiration and finally the determination. However, from his own experience he was convinced that in order to carry out a given task one can surely do away with mood and inspiration and straightway concentrate on determination.

History wise he was not the only one to propound Nastik philosophy. The people of his genre (Nastik) have existed through the ages. The problem is only their microscopic minority. The exponents of Astik School of thought being in majority have so organized the world that generations of people go on joining them without a murmur. So much so, despite Nastik philosophy being very old in India, no text is available on it and it is preserved only in the writings, which tried to negate or criticize it.

Now something about the overwhelming Astik school of thought! Good people among the Astiks, must be some exceptions few and far between. What one finds is that most of them follow double standards in day-to-day life, believing and deceiving their so-called God in every action. First, they are not unanimous on the forms of God and how he created the world. Then the plethora of religions and contradictory religious practices and rituals aimed at pleasing God. Less said the better. All the religions preach love for humanity, but most of their followers limit their love, only to their co-religionists. Not only that, there are sects and sub-sects within every religion, old and new, which remain in perpetual state of conflict with each other, often indulging in orgies ofbloodshed. By the way, are we all not aware that history wise religion is the single biggest cause of bloodshed in the whole world? Further down the line are the dubious means of existence in every society at individual, family, community, state, and country levels, where by hoodwinking and treachery, blatant and concealed, are in vogue. While the ruling classes all over the world justify their bad actions as politics or diplomacy, the common people call such actions as professionalism.

Concentrating on the Indian scene, there is no dearth of blatant double standards and dishonesty at all levels among the Astiks. There are our politicians swearing by the holy Constitution of India and building fortunes by misusing their Constitutional position. There are spineless bureaucrats dancing to the tunes of their political masters and making fast buck. There are government officials getting promotions and other benefits over the heads of their colleagues and seniors, and doing little work. There are countless people evading taxes, and defrauding the nation in various ways. There are judges selling 'justice' for a price. There are doctors of government hospitals making money through private practice. There are manufacturers of spurious drugs. There are teachers illegally giving home tuitions. There are others, who steal electricity, travel without ticket, and adulterate eatables and other consumables for easy money. There are those who print or deal in fake currency. There are those who smuggle and sell narcotics. There are those who throw garbage on public roads, parks and other open places causing stench and disease. There are those who break queue at hospital, railway station, bus stand, bank, post-office, billing office etc. There are those who encroach upon the roads and streets causing traffic bottlenecks. There are 'halwaees' weighing cardboard box along with 'mithaee'. There are those who build places of worship to grab public lands for commercial use. There are those who steal money from donation boxes of religious places. There are 'religious-minded' government officials who use their official vehicles to visit places of worship. There are those who disturb others with religious functions of various kinds, day in and day out. There are saints and 'babas' accused of indulging in immoral activities including flesh trade and rape. There are those who kill their daughters and sisters for marrying the men of their choice. A chairman of Punjab Public Service Commission makes millions in jobs-for-money scam. A flying club boss makes flying licenses against illegal gratification. A 'baba' running an orphanage is accused of 'illegal' sale of his dead wards' eyes. Another 'baba' misappropriates huge 'Kaar Sewa' funds for personal gains. An army Major stages fake encounter with Pakistani army in J&K for rewards. A politician stashes ill-gotten cash in the 'pujaroom' of his house. A 'DGP' is arrested for receiving illegal gratification in Maharashtra. A 'Shankracharya' is accused of murder. A chief Minister conspires to siphon away millions in a fodder scam. A retired DGP is convicted of molesting a girl of his daughter's age and has to surrender the President's Police Medal granted to him for 'meritorious service'. A president of Medical Council of India is arrested along with accomplices for receiving twenty million rupees as bribe to grant an illegal favour to a private medical college located in Punjab. All confirmed Astiks! Shame, shame!! And the tragedy is that none of their co-religionists has ever come forward to denounce them for violation of so called religious norms.

A myth that Astiks blatantly propound to camouflage their misdeeds, is that everyone pays for his misdeeds. Examples are given of those who indulged in corruption and faced punishment later or suffered in some other way. But, there are countless others who go unpunished. In fact, in the words of Khushwant Singh, 'there are many who do not suffer any pangs of guilt, remain in good health, eat well, live well, enjoy life and esteem of their fellow citizens, send their children to the best schools and colleges and see them fixed in plum jobs and married into rich families which ensures their future prospects'. Do all those bigwigs feel any guilt for squandering public money on weddings in their families? What justification do our politicians and bureaucrats have for amassing wealth worth millions by misusing their official positions? By the way they all claim to be followers of this or that religious faith. Again in the words of Khushwant Singh, 'they must be having explanations to have peace of mind, but to say that they would suffer for their sins, may be in their next lives as well, is just hoodwinking'.

* * *

Chapter 21

The telephone rang frantically that Monday evening of June, when he was in the bath on return from office. Sapna and Parody were away those days to look after their ailing sister in Delhi. As a result, the job of cooking, cleaning, and washing took a lot of his time, leaving almost no spare moments. How he wished Sapna to return to save him from the drudgery, and so much for the missing sexual bliss!

The telephone rang again for long, when he was busy in the kitchen after the bath and avoided to pick up the receiver, lest the dish he was preparing got burnt.

The ring came again at bedtime and he picked up the receiver, after the ring did not stop for too long.

"O my God, you are home! Where were you all the while? I hope you have not forgotten us."

The female voice at the other end was terse and appeared to be familiar. Why his wife should speak so to him, he thought, especially when he had returned from long leave back home in Punjab only two weeks earlier, and had spoken to her on phone barely the day before. May be it was a 'wrong number' he presumed, and thought of telling so to the caller. But, he decided not to.

So, in a double mind he blurted a non-committal 'hello' and pat came a question, "How are you going on with your morning walk and 'shavasan' these days?"

"Oh me!" It suddenly dawned upon him, it was Rachni calling after about two years, and he said loudly into the receiver, "Very nicely. How you and your son?"

Pat came her reply again, "Both fine and kicking," followed by 'Namaskar'.

"Namaskar," he repeated and asked, "What can I do for you?"

Then in a barely audible voice as if speaking in confidence, Rachni told him, she was sending a visitor, whom she had "permitted" to stay with him.

"What for?" He asked and she replied, "For 31-day puja."

"O my . . . What are you up to . . . ?" He asked, and she said, "Listen to me!"

Then giving the details, Rachni told that the visitor was the daughter of her mother-in-law's sister. The girl was too close to her and having fallen on bad days for no fault of hers, needed help. She was about to be thrown out by her rich marital family for not bearing a child, and that the 31-day 'puja' at the 'Temple of Fertility' was her last chance.

"There are many coming to the temple every year. Why bother?" He said.

"But, she is special my dear! I have chosen her to stay with you, and receive your guidance and help for the success of her 'puja'. The nourishing drink, the 'shavasan', and the mantra for increasing self-confidence, I mean. She lives in my neighbourhood. She is ready to undergo any type of penance. I am sending her to you as my right to help the needy through you. Besides, I want to keep my mother-in-law under obligation by helping her sister's daughter beget a child." Rachni spoke with authority.

"What . . . if . . . ?" He blurted.

"Nothing doing! She leaves by train tomorrow and the 'puja' begins on Friday, the day of 'purnima.'"

"Let her come, but how do I know her mind . . . ?"

"Well, that's for you to find out. A product of the puritanical society and orthodox to the core, she is certainly a hard nut to crack. I have only given her an idea that you can also help her for sure success, and that the 'puja' may become irrelevant under your treatment, which begins with psychotherapy. May be, you also need to strengthen your self-confidence, to convince her to take your remedy. I am sending her to you with fond hopes. I may only tell you; this is in my interest. I want a child to play with my son, and a woman with whom I can share my feelings about you . . . I mean. Yes or no?"

"What if I do not succeed and she spills the beans of your success?"

"Well, you have to take it as a challenge, for the sake of one, whom you have logically accepted as your wife! Is a husband not duty-bound to fulfil the wishes of his wife besides safeguarding her honour and dignity? Did Rama not go to hunt the elusive deer at the instance of Sita, knowing fully well the outcome? Have I not surrendered my womanly possessions to you as your wife? How can you morally afford to let me down? Any how, I assure you, I have full faith in your prowess at rationalised seduction!" Rachni said, and banged the receiver with a lovely 'Namaskar', just leaving him in a trauma.

However, recovering soon, he visualised the coming events with a positive mind and found himself preparing to convince an orthodox woman to adopt an un-orthodox path to 'live honourably'. He also marvelled at Rachni for throwing a formidable challenge to him, which if gone awry, could ruin her own life as well.

So, the challenge facing him was two-pronged. One, he had to seduce an unknown woman to surrender her womanly possessions to the adulterous male-pig in him, in return for help to hoodwink the egocentric society whose self-seeking members were blind to her problems. Two, he had to ensure success at 'seduction' to save the honour of Rachni who had reposed her confidence in him with fond hopes as his 'wife'.

* * *

Chapter 22

It was Wednesday. He was about to leave for office, when the doorbell rang in an unfamiliar manner. Opening the door, he found a woman of small stature, with a heavy carry bag placed by her side. She was wearing a costly silken 'sari' of light green colour. With child-like innocence playing on her face, at the very first look she appeared to be more a girl in the middle of her late teens, than a married woman, but for her 'bindi' and the vermilion mark. Her breasts were heavier and hip-zone disproportionately bigger, as compared to the totality of her appearance. With 'Ajanta' features on a round face and the stout ashy complexion, she looked sweet. A voice told him from within, "She is beauty-in-distress and in dire need of your help!"

"So, you have come. Why are you late? Train time is so early." He asked in one go.

However, without caring to reply, she secured the 'pallu' of her 'sari' on her head, and offered hand-folded 'Namaskar' with lowered eyes. He had no way to react other than reciprocating the 'Namaskar' with a caring pat on her left shoulder.

As he was to leave for office, he ushered the guest in, pointed at the room for her to stay, and left saying, "I will be back by the evening only. Take care."

On his return from office in the evening, he found a lot of change. The house had been dusted, clothes washed and the kitchen put in proper order. Not only this, the woman herself was unrecognisable in T-shirt and a slit-skirt. The T-shirt showed the curves of her big and braless breasts, while the skirt almost exposed her shapely thighs.

With a 'Namaskar' in welcome, she led him to the sofa in his room and left to reappear soon with a glass of water. As he lifted the glass, she bent forward slightly and asked, "Tea, coffee or juice please?"

"As you like." He said and reclined on the sofa with the glass of water in hand.

"No, the order needs to be specific." She said and stood erect.

Happy at her exposition he said, "Juice please!"

Then going with calculated steps, she returned with two tumblers of juice and some snacks. Lifting his tumbler, he beckoned her to take the other. She happily obliged and took a seat across the table facing him.

Taking juice, he suddenly felt there was something odd about his guest whose name he was yet to ask. Yes, it was her trimmed hair, which made her look odd and more girlish.

"I am sorry, but what is your name?" He asked his sweet guest with the last sip.

"Leela . . . . My name is Leela Devi. But they called me Leeloo in childhood. In fact my mother and father still address me as Leeloo."

"A lovely name! But I would like to call you Dolly. Why not! You look like a beautiful doll! Yes . . . Take my word!"

"Am I . . . ? Really . . . ? But in the face of my problem, I feel as if this beauty is of no use at all."

"May be, you have been to college. Hope I am right. Am I?"

"Yes, you are right. I was almost through my M.A. (History), when they plucked me from the college and married me off. And . . . that made me a miserable wife. At the mercy of my in-laws. Our society is such. Nothing doing!"

"Who says, you are a miserable wife at the mercy of your in-laws? Your society could be what it is. But you are certainly not miserable. Take my word again for that."

"I do not get you, but presently I am getting late for my evening 'puja' at the temple which I have set up in my room. By the way, when do I call you for dinner?"

"May be at nine." He said becoming specific and she went to her room.

* * *

Chapter 23

He gave due praise to Dolly for the dinner, of course with the intention to get her talking. But he failed.

"How do you say I am not miserable?" Dolly ultimately opened her mouth, when they were about to rise after dinner.

"Yes, there is no doubt in what I have said. In my view, miserable is the person whose problem is beyond solution, and I feel for sure, your problem is not beyond solution. Of course, you may have some reservations about the solution, which I visualise you can certainly get rid of, to change your life for the better. Hence you are not miserable."

"I don't get you at all. Please tell me clearly what you want to say."

"Okay, let us put it like this. First, you will tell me how and why do you feel miserable?"

"Yes. I am a woman, very much dubbed in India as the weaker sex. That means I am living at the mercy of the man; the stronger sex. It is the man, man, and the man every where! The man controls the family and the man controls the society. On parental side are father and brothers, and on the marital side are father-in-law and husband besides brothers-in-law in control, later joined by sons and nephews: all men. The woman on both sides plays subservient role: always at the mercy of men. Always saying ditto to what the men say or do. Always helpless and miserable! And so am I! Helpless and miserable!"

"That I feel is the generalised version of your problem in the face of which you feel helpless, and consequently miserable. That is the outcome of the society as a whole in our country. What I want to know is your specific problem."

"Well, my problem is very serious. I was born and brought up in a rich family and educated at that. I was married to a person, no doubt financially well off. But, I am his second wife. The first one was hounded out of the house for not bearing a child within five years of marriage. And now it seems my turn to be hounded out. It is already fourth year to the marriage, but no child. This 31-day 'puja' is the last chance."

"Are you sure you will beget a child with this 31-day 'puja'?"

"Well, I have come with the hope. Actually, it may or may not be. But, Rachni 'didi' told me you could also help for sure success. I don't know how."

"Yes, I can certainly help. Yes, I can! Take my word once again! And so I say, you are not miserable! But for that, you may have to take a rational decision."

"What decision is required on my part and how would it help me?"

"By the way, what do you think, could be the reason of your not begetting a child?"

"May be it is my fate, and so they say."

"How do you think this 'puja' would help you?"

"Well, God is great, and I have full faith in God!"

"May be if you want my help, you will have to have faith in yourself, rather than what you call God."

"Is it? But every body believes in God! The creator of us all!"

"That is why I say, you need to take a rational decision. For a beginning, you will have to forget what others feel or say. That is the scientific key to your success rather than the blind faith."

"You may be right, but where does all this take me?"

"Coming to your problem once again, may I ask whether you and your husband are medically and biologically fit and compatible to produce a child?"

"Yes, I am fit. The doctor declared me fit for bearing a child. But my husband is not ready for the test. May be due to ego."

"I feel your problem is identical with that of Rachni. But I wonder if . . ." Anyhow you may go to sleep now."

"But that still takes me no where. Do you think it is possible for me to sleep with my thought process in a state of uncertainty?"

"Well, there is no harm in trying. You have come to try the 31-day 'puja' with uncertainty of success and you can try to sleep under conditions of uncertainty as well. What you need to decide under conditions of uncertainty is the method you would like to adopt for solution of your problem. Should it be the 'puja' with uncertain result, for which you have come all the way? Should you take my remedy with sure success as hinted by your 'didi'? And very sure, you can decide this issue only while trying to sleep under conditions of uncertainty with no one around to disturb."

That seemed to have convinced her and she went to her room.

* * *

Chapter 24

Nothing of importance was discussed next morning. By the time he returned from office in the evening, Dolly had already paid a familiarity-visit to the 'Temple of Fertility', and put on the customary calf-length 'bhagwa-chola'. After coffee, she went in for her evening 'puja', and called him for dinner in due course.

She took his praise for the dinner almost silently. Ultimately not able to bear her silence, he asked why she was serious.

"I have some questions to ask, but I fail to find words." She said.

"Come on. Do not feel shy. Are you ready for the 31-day 'puja' beginning tomorrow?" He prompted her to speak.

"Yes, I am ready. As you see, I have already changed into the 'puja' gear with this 'bhagwa-chola', discarding the worldly clothes. I know the 'puja' is tiring. And the day-time 'maun'!"

"Never mind. Hard work is the key to success, they say."

"Yes, that is so. But, what if I don't get what I want out of the 'puja', despite putting in what you call hard work?"

"Your problem has a solution! But for that, you need not discard the 'puja', at least for the time being."

"What solution do you have for my problem? I want to know immediately."

"Well, for that, you need to have a strong mind. Every human being has something called mind which has unlimited energy. The need is only to utilise that hidden energy. For that matter, the hidden energy has to be recognised and channelled for the desired use."

"I feel you are becoming mysterious by the minute. Why don't you tell me every thing clearly?"

"So you are very serious!"

"Yes, if you feel so."

"Okay. Please do not mind my plain speaking. You are educated enough to understand the stark realities of life. I am afraid to say, your husband may not be biologically fit and compatible with you. If he were, you could not have been here."

"Where is the solution of my problem in what you say?"

"It is in your mind. It depends upon your mind's ability to choose between living honourably by bearing a child and being hounded out of your home for want of a child. As the things stand with your husband being unfit and incompatible, I dare say, you can beget a child only by mating with a man other than your husband. That is why I say you are not miserable. But the decision has to be yours. It is only the matter of survival by getting better of the society and the so-called stronger sex, in the race of life. This is called 'survival instinct' as well. Get my point?"

"Impossible! Beyond ethics! I come from a respectable background! Why should I carry a bastard?"

"Well, you can marry the man of your choice as well, to convince your sense of ethics. You are a student of history. You know, polygamy and polyandry both have remained in vogue in our society and culture through ages and may be these are still in practice in some communities. No?"

"Your guidance is no doubt philosophic. But, I wonder if the proposed solution would be justified in the pretentious society from where I come!"

"Where is the need of giving justification to such a society, which is blind to your problem? Why go public about a personal matter in which the public has no sympathy for you? It is the matter of your survival. What justification does your husband have in turning you out of your home, for no fault of yours? Why should he spoil your life for his ego? Why should you suffer for others' whims? If your marital family can be so harsh, why cannot you devise a way out to negate that harshness? Anyhow, this is only a suggestion. You may give a thought to it in due course. For the time being, you should only concentrate on your 'puja' beginning tomorrow."

"What a silly situation!" Dolly remarked with a long sigh, and went to her room.

Next morning, Friday, Dolly was a bit tense when she left for the 'Temple of Fertility'. He went to the office as usual, but returned at lunchtime, to prepare the nourishing drink, which he had served to Rachni three years back.

The bell rang at last, and he went to the door almost running. Dolly was perspiring and dog-tired, as expected. Rather, her condition was more pitiable than Rachni's, on the first day of 'puja'. As she almost fell on the bed in his room, his heart went out to her. What for such a sweet little thing was suffering the torture of 31-day 'puja', he asked himself. Very much concerned with her condition, he increased the fan speed and instructed her to take deep breathing. When he returned with the nourishing drink, she almost snatched the glass. Taking more than usual time in finishing a glassful, she slowly stretched herself on the bed with 'now what' look in her eyes.

Per plan, he made her adopt 'shavasan'. Guiding her to relax from toes onward, he felt like consoling her with an affectionate kiss on her forehead, but some how managed to restrain himself. The mantra he gave her was the same as given to Rachni. Soon, she was fully relaxed and sleeping.

She was really fresh and vigorous when she emerged out of his room after a bath after sunset. Almost impulsively, he offered juice to her, which she accepted willingly, and sat across the dining table, to sip. Next two days being his weekend holidays, he served the drink and guided Dolly to sleep in 'shavasan', repeating the mantra of self-confidence. From Monday onward, she became expert enough to take care of herself and everything got going well.

*   *   *

Chapter 25

On coming Saturday the change occurred, when Dolly came out of his room after sunset and was sitting in front of him, with the glass of juice in hand.

Half way through the juice, she got going with the question, "Are you sure, I'll beget a child with your plan?"

"Why not? Only the need on your part is to act with self-confidence. To decide . . . I mean to say."

"May be I . . . already . . . decision!"

"So?"

"May be . . . I . . . marriage! I do not want to bear an illegitimate child. No?"

"So, you have chosen to live honourably!"

"Can I plan the marriage for tomorrow?"

"Yes, but where is your man?"

"I am no fool. Who can be my man, other than my guide-philosopher himself? No?"

"Are you sure?"

"Yes, I am very sure. Now that I have the opportunity calling, it would be a folly on my part to let it go unchallenged. No?"

"Well, how do you plan to solemnise the marriage?"

"Very simple. I shall formally accept my guide-philosopher as my husband in a brief ceremony. That would be followed by a marriage-feast to be hosted by me for the two of us, and then 'my husband' physically carries me to the bedchamber for 'suhagraat', as per custom. All events in a chain, one after the other, tomorrow evening. No?"

"Any help you need from me?"

"No. There is nothing so difficult to manage. I shall visit a boutique in the neighbourhood tomorrow afternoon and make other necessary arrangements".

"What about some guests as witnesses?"

"No need at all. Why make public an affair, which is strictly between the two of us? For that matter, I feel this house of yours will be the most appropriate witness. No?"

"Yes, I get your point. But, I have one more question. What about your 'puja', for which you have come all the way? I ask that because I may not allow you as my wife to waste energy on such useless things as 'puja' to beget a child."

"May be, my 'puja' is here now, rather than the temple!"

"Congrats! And what about favouring your would be husband with pre-marriage celebration today?"

"No problem, now that the path is visible! But I would like to be the host for the pre-marriage celebration as well."

"The 'Somras'? Do you . . . ?"

"No problem again. I have seen the stock in your cupboard. No?"

The 'pre-marriage celebration' got going after Dolly came to his room with a loaded tray and poured 'Royal Challenge' whisky in two glasses. Sitting by his side with her body language denoting full surrender, she looked fascinating in her 'bhagwa-chola'.

"How do we get going with the celebration?" She asked after pouring the drinks.

"May be, with a sweet kiss on your lovely cheek." He said, placing his hand on her shoulder.

"You are so seductive . . . !" She said, and brought her face closer.

After kissing her for the first time, he raised the glass with, "Cheers to Dolly, my would be wife!"

"Cheers to my guide-philosopher and chosen biological mate!" Dolly said, and exchanging the glasses, they settled for 'pre-marriage celebration' or so to say the night-before-marriage.

He had no problem unzipping Dolly's 'chola' at the back after two rounds of whisky. Fondling the curves of her body, he found she was hard enough. Her breasts and buttocks were firm, despite being outsized, and four years of her marriage.

There was no problem either, making her sit on his lap. Her surrender was so complete, that by the time they finished the dinner, libido had fully taken over both of them and soon there was a pillow under the hips of naked Dolly on the bed.

Sprawling with half-closed eyes and hands placed on the outsized domes of her breasts as a gesture of shyness, she did not seem to be having even an iota of guilt in her body language.

Her parted thighs, as well as the two high-rise hemispheres of her breasts appeared to be longing for early action on his part. Her vaginal fissure was self-lubricated from the flared-up passion and with every thing in place, the male-pig in him jubilantly launched the assault. So, it was a treat for him to mount the drunken Dolly and push his thick glans penis into her 'labia minora' with slight pressure of thumb.

"Wait, wait . . ." Dolly said, almost trying to get free, halfway through his pushing action.

"Are you kidding?" He asked, stopping the pushing action but keeping her in place.

"No! I am afraid! Really! It may be painful for me to have the whole lot inside! It is so big and hard!" She almost begged.

"Okay. Let us relax as we are." He comforted her.

"How caring of you!" She murmured with a tug of her hand on his back.

"How do you feel now?" He asked after caressing her for a while.

"May be a bit comfortable! But, no going further! Please! I am still afraid!"

"May be your fears are false! You seem to be experiencing the maleness in full form for the first time".

"Yes, you are right! I never knew it could be of such big dimensions."

"What about your formal husband?"

"A tame affair! It is all hush-hush with him. Let me forget him for the time being. Please!"

May be, some more cuddling was required to take Dolly further 'up the golden path'. So, he took to fondling her breasts and twitching the sensual nipples, besides uttering endearments, and affectionately burying his teeth on the left and right sides of her neck. Doing so, he found Dolly soon muttering sweet nothings and straining her legs inward.

Then he felt, the convulsions of her vaginal muscles indicating that her sexual climax might not be very far; when the eternal female feels like taking the whole eternal male into herself.

Judging the coming event from experience, he adjusted his elbows on her left and right and gripped her shoulders with both hands. As expected, in a few moments he found her bracing up her hips after sidewise turning her head: an excellent opportunity for him to act.

"O . . . my . . . Dolly . . . !" He muttered, and making speedy and firm hip-jerks, pushed the whole male-shaft into the tight slot between her thighs. While he kept the 'joint' from getting abruptly dislocated, her climax came calling.

Thus, with the ideal becoming reality, Dolly's body quivered for some time in his tight embrace, and calmed down. Remaining motionless in that position, he allowed her to come to grips with the full male entry and again took to hugging and fondling her.

Stimulated by his love-play and shower of sweet nothings, she composed herself in a short while shedding false fears, and began responding to his pushing and pulling, with sensual hissing and whining.

As the tempo of his thrusts went on, sending waves of sexual excitement through her nervous system, Dolly changed over to uncontrollable shrieks and shrills, reminding him of Sapna.

So, riding the waves of his success at leading an orthodox woman to take an unorthodox path in the race of life, he maintained the speed of his up-down motions in fits and starts, until he found Dolly bracing up for another climax. That, he felt was the moment for him to sow his seed in the waiting furrow, and so he increased the speed of his thrusts from 'camel's walk' to the 'horse's gallop'. With that broke a storm inside his loins sending bursts of semen into the depths of his ladylove, who reciprocated with striving to lift her hips, and sensual hissing. Ultimately, the tide of passion subsided as it should, and in the prevailing lull, they fell motionless clinging to each other like creepers.

No doubt, the indulgence was enjoyable for both of them, and they were at it until wee hours, of course with usual halts and talk-sessions replete with hissing sounds.

* * *

Chapter 26

Sunday, the day of marriage was marvellous. Dolly woke him up from a sound sleep in the forenoon and after a bath and brunch, he went to sleep again. At about 4.00 pm, he got up and again took a bath. Finding Dolly off to the market, he took his afternoon coffee and got busy in the newspapers of the day behind closed door.

Lo and behold! At 6.15 pm, Dolly appeared in his room with a bang! She was in a bridal dress with tribal tinge; decorated with artificial flowers and beads of various colours. Her face was in 'ghungat' and she was carrying the customary 'thali'. In order to play his part well in the coming ceremony, he had prepared a makeshift garland of currency notes without her knowledge.

Placing the 'thali' on the table, Dolly offered a hand-folded 'Namaskar' and sat in front of him. Offering herself in marriage to him, she honoured him with a garland, performed his 'arti', and gave him a palm-date to eat. Uncovering her face in acceptance, he put vermilion mark in the parting of her hair, honoured her with the garland of currency notes, gave her sweetmeat to eat, and kissed her forehead. Then in congratulation, they lifted glasses of coconut milk. The ceremony was simple and brief, but convincing.

Dolly arranged the 'marriage feast' in the lobby-cum-dining room, where she invited him about an hour after the 'marriage ceremony'. When he went there, he was just amazed! The location was decorated with buntings and flowers. The dining table was lined with eating and drinking material. Dolly was standing behind a decorated chair at the head of the dining table. There was nothing on her body, but for a 'mukut' of flowers on head, and a lavishly embroidered yellow 'odhni' hanging from the neck over to her frontals, and secured at the waist with a flower belt.

Coming into action on his arrival, the 'bride' ushered him on to the decorated chair, showered rose petals on him, and poured a drink.

Encircling her waist with his left arm, he raised the glass in the name of "A fruitful married life for both of us," took a double sip, and gave a double sip to her. Then placing the glass on the table, he took Dolly in a tight embrace and showered kisses on her. Recovering from the embrace, she took the nearest seat on his side, and the marriage feast commenced.

During the feast, he managed to throw away the 'odhni' of Dolly after a couple of joint pegs, to watch her in the nude! At his instance, she also gave naked dance performance to the tune of an audio player. Dancing in the nude in gay abandon, she was no less than the beauties dancing in the annual carnival of the Samba dancers of Rio de Janeiro. With whisky telling upon her system, she also became bold enough to remind him a few times, to physically carry her to the bedchamber after the feast, 'as per custom'.

The 'marriage feast' continued for fairly long, with the bride acting as the host. With so much of eating and drinking, there was no need of a formal dinner. So, by about 10pm he thought it was time for him to take over.

When he entered the bedchamber physically carrying the naked Dolly in drunken state after the feast, there was another surprise. The bed had a milky-white sheet with rose petals lavishly scattered on it. At the centre of the bed was a pillow with the legend "WELCOME" in embroidery. Dolly had been moving in and out of the bedroom during the feast on the pretext of showing her nakedness to him. However, it was just beyond his comprehension that she could be up to all this. It was really very nice of her, to make the 'suhagraat' so memorable!

With no other formality left, he put his bride on the bed with her outsized buttocks on the 'welcome pillow'. Then, settling between her parted legs, he nibbled at her nipples for a while and inserted the head of his throbbing male shaft into her waiting pussy. Ready to cooperate in the game of love, she encircled his lower thighs with her legs. His hip-jerks were slow and calculated in the beginning. Nevertheless, with about half the entry, Dolly seemed to be responding lustily under intoxication. With such an enthusiastic welcome, he suddenly increased the pushing force and drove the whole shaft into the self-lubricated slot almost in one go. That sent her into a sort of spin action and she moved her head left and right under the bursting pressure from within. However, with his grip preventing her from dislocating and her excited libido forcing her to enjoy the situation, she was able to compose herself soon. Not only did she soon compose herself, but also threw a flying kiss towards him, as if prompting him to begin the up-down motion of his hips.

During the coming three weeks or so, it was 'honeymoon at home', for all intents and purposes!

The postures of intercourse tried on day-to-day basis were many. But, 'three-in-one' turned out to be their favourite. That began with Dolly going 'on-all-the-fours', whereby he sent the male-shaft into her vagina from back, standing on the floor by bedside as in blue movies. After some time changing the position to 'the-woman-atop-man', Dolly sat facing him with her parted legs, at his middle. In that position, invariably they shared a drink leisurely, which Dolly liked very much. The finale was always brought about with 'Punjabi posture' as reflected in the reply given by an enthusiastic Punjabi to an Englishman's question. 'How do you do?' 'Sir, we in Punjab, generally do by placing both her legs on the shoulders.' Hi! Hi!

As all good things tend to have a short life, so this 'honeymoon' ended soon, and Dolly was off at the end of her supposed 31-day 'puja'. The confirmation about the pregnancy came soon through a joint phone call made by Rachni and Dolly, and in due course Dolly gave birth to twins: a beautiful son and a beautiful daughter.

When Dolly came along with the twins for her '10-day thanks giving puja', she had two more companions: Rachni and her son! During their stay with him, he got leave from office to be with his extended family on 24-hour basis. Enjoying the marital bliss with his two 'wives' for about two weeks, he found both of them as obedient and loving to him, and very friendly to each other. While Dolly took over the task of looking after the kitchen as well as the children, Rachni remained almost glued to him, day and night. Their daytime dresses were formal and costly, but they invariably appeared for dinner in tribal dresses, showing their pristine nakedness. The drinks were taken just as appetiser avoiding excess and there was no jealousy between the co-sisters. Their pass time after dinner was to sit on the sofa by his sides: watching television, and rubbing their bodies on his sides. Some times Dolly suckled her twins sitting in the nude presenting a perfect mother's picture. Rachni's naughty son generally played havoc with the house and often barged into the main bedroom: playing, playing and playing; unaware of what her mother could be up to.

Being recently through delivery, Dolly did not evince much interest in sex and rightly so. Successful at living honourably as per his plan, she was in fact in a thanks-giving mood and free from all kinds of anxiety. Similarly being thankful to Rachni also for guiding her to him, she had adopted the path of service to both of them. So it was mainly Rachni, who accompanied him on the sexual odysseys, with Dolly happily watching and providing moral support to both of them.

"What if you beget a child out of this visit also?" He asked Rachni one night during copulation.

"That's my wish of course! My body temperature is slightly higher since yesterday and this time I want a baby girl. For a balanced family! That is. Yes or no?"

Hearing the reply, he placed her legs on his shoulders in the 'Punjabi' way, which made her issue the cries of excitement. That attracted the attention of Dolly in the kitchen, and she came running as if to the aid of her co-sister. Anyhow, at the 'All Okay' signal from Rachni, she left back: smiling. So strange are the ways of sensuality! Believe me or not! Really!

*   *   *

Chapter 27

The rickety parody of a girl that he had seen on her first visit to his house, developed into a buxom beauty, by the time she passed high school with first division around seventeen years of her age. There after, her education stopped, and door-to-door domestic jobs became whole-day affair for her. She was no doubt, very intelligent and fit for higher education. But, she had to take up domestic jobs instead, for want of financial support, and general lack of opportunities for the 'deserving' in India. Otherwise, what could have she done in the paradox of a country named India, where political short-sightedness and organised-corruption rule supreme? Yes, political short-sightedness and organised corruption, I say! Well that is India with no holds barred and thriving with scandals and scams in every sphere! Examples? Less said the better!

Anyhow, with Parody coming of age, her elder sister took to making frantic efforts to find a suitable husband for her. Often during those days, Sapna told him, about having found and rejected this or that matrimonial proposal for her younger sister, who she said was 'very dear' to her. She also took to making purchases of goodies for the marriage in advance, and frequently gave her savings to him for safe custody, only to take away the same abruptly, to make purchases.

For almost seven years of Parody visiting his house, the polygamous male-pig in him, did not ever nurse the vision of an amorous relationship with her. The idea took shape in his mind, with a chance seeing her under shower. It happened by the end of the seventh year.

In fact, with the passage of time, Parody had been taking him so much for granted; she never expected any thing 'wrong' on his part. That was, because she had always found him keeping to himself unless provoked. Daily visiting his house for the 'wholesome breakfast', she would often go without even speaking to him beyond hand-folded 'Namaskar'. Despite being liberal in many ways, he used to speak to her, only when she asked, and remained busy in his own affairs when not disturbed.

It was late forenoon on a humid holiday, when he was busy in the balcony and Parody came for work in place of her elder sister: Sapna. She gave him a glass of water at his instance and took to her job without disturbing him.

After some time, unaware of what Parody could be doing, he got up and went to the bedroom to pick up a book, and there it was!

It happened so unexpected and so sudden, that he was taken aback at the very sight of it, and wanted to run out of the bedroom.

But, the omnivorous male-pig from his within prompted him to have another look.

There she was! A buxom beauty! In the nude under shower! In his attached bathroom!

Her back was to the door, which perhaps she had not cared to close, taking for granted that he would keep sitting as always in the balcony, where he was that day.

On the second look, he could not take his eyes off the feast, and sank in a chair! Wide-eyed!! Watching!!!

The beauty under shower had already soaped her chiselled granite body, and was slowly rubbing it. She was taking slow turns, left and right, to ensure proper wash. As she turned and twisted under the falling water, he could clearly see her hands; moving on her hips and narrow waist, and then cupping the lovely pair of breasts and alternately bringing the two honey pots under direct shower.

"... Vow! What a view ... !"

"... Par excellence ... !"

"... Water melting from a nude virgin's face and shoulders ... !"

"... Down to the lovely breasts, belly-button, pubic-pad, and the hidden love-pot ... !"

"... And cascading over the corpulent hips and shapely thighs to the floor below ... !"

"... Making sounds like muffled jingle-bells ... !"

"... Unpolluted beauty ... !"

"... A blooming flower ... !"

"... Nature at its best ... !"

"... What a shape ... !"

"... An 'ashata-dhatu' idol ... !"

"... Vibrating and pulsating ... !"

"... In flesh and blood ... !"

"... Lavishly handsome ... !"

"... Tantalizing and tempting ... !"

"... Titillating ... !"

"... Mesmerizing ... !"

"... What a total transformation from what I had seen seven years back ... !"

"Oh ... ! Oh ... !"

"... . ! ... !"

While he was watching wonderstruck with his consciousness crowded with amorous thoughts like a pit of snakes, the view was suddenly lost to him.

Oh! It vanished as quickly as it had emerged!

Because, sensing his presence, 'the beauty in the bath' gave him a sheepish look, and snap-closed the bathroom door!

No doubt, her action was the one expected from an average Indian girl of her age and upbringing. Yet an idea took shape in his mind, with possibility of one day transforming into action!

The idea?

Yes, the idea!

The idea was to hold the buxom beauty in the nude to his chest with a pillow under her hips, and adjust his hip-zone between her parted thighs. And ... and ... !

Well, that was the time, when Parody had crossed eighteen, and Sapna had confided in him, about pursuing a matrimonial proposal for her, through a go-between, with the son of a distant relative living at Kolkata. She claimed that the targeted family was in the real estate business, and financially well placed. She told that once married into that family, the girl would no longer have to take up domestic jobs; living happily thereafter. She also said that Kolkata being a far off place, she would certainly miss her younger sister very much after marriage, adding in the same breath that the future comfortable life of the girl would certainly suffice for separation.

In fact, Sapna seemed to be very much confident about the proposed alliance coming through. Her main worry, however, was the money required for the marriage ceremony to match the status of the groom's family. It was with this in mind that she one day asked him if he could loan some money to her in the event of the marriage taking place suddenly. And he assured her to do the needful.

During the year or so following the bathroom incident, Parody further improved upon the tantalizing curves of her body and developed into a captivating beauty with sleepy slanting eyes, while her elder sister became increasingly worried about her marriage.

In confidence, Parody too told him, about her elder sister's resolve to select a good family groom from Kolkata for her. She also became increasingly beauty conscious, perhaps with the desire to match the good financial status of her proposed marital family.

With the passage of time it so happened that the thought of Parody's marriage became an all-pervasive obsession for the two sisters. Explaining the mania one day, Sapna told him that in her community, girls were married off maximum by the age of sixteen as per custom. By that yardstick, she said, her younger sister around nineteen had since crossed the age of marriage, and that it was becoming more and more difficult to find a desirable match for her with every passing day. She told that she had herself been married off during the seventeenth year of her age, and the first child was born to her during the eighteenth.

As such, he felt, the worries of Sapna were genuine, and so he had all the sympathies for her over this issue. Also, the official marriage age for girls in India being eighteen years,

Parody had already crossed the qualifying mark, and so had every right to anticipate the event. The urgency was also justified in view of the fact that she was expecting to get rid of the drudgery of the door-to-door jobs after marriage.

* * *

Chapter 28

With every passing month, his visits to the city markets along with Parody increased. That was at the instance of Sapna: to help Parody make purchases for her marriage, which had not yet been fixed but appeared imminent.

May be it was in recognition of his help to select suitable goodies for her marriage, when Parody gave the most cherished remarks in his favour one day.

"From outside my family, I regard your love for me as the most intense." She said.

While she could have given these remarks just out of her innocence, the male chauvinistic pig in him seemed to be having specific plans. This was so, because, with every passing day, the bathroom incident occupied more and more of his mind, and the thought of her nakedness had become a passion with him. As a result, at every mention of her marriage, he visualized some unknown person getting the right to disrobe her, and score her body contours without fear.

Ultimately, after prolonged consultations, Parody's proposed alliance with the Kolkata boy came through. Soon it transpired that her family was going to Kolkata to perform the marriage ceremony, as the groom's family had so desired. With this development, Parody became anxious to leave for the 'Promised Land', while his heart became heavier and heavier.

With the departure coming near day by day, he visualized the bird flying out of his hands, and perching on some other person's shoulder.

May be it was his anxiety, which, with a gust of passion in his bedroom about fifteen days before Parody's departure for Kolkata, propelled him to place his hands on her shoulders, and plant a kiss on her cheek, despite her hesitation.

But, that was not to be, as she seemed to be stunned with his action.

Anyway, taking her stance as the superfluous show of vanity before surrender, he tried to pull her closer to him; to press her bosom against his.

But, she abruptly plucked herself off him, and darted out of the house, leaving him nonplussed.

After that incident, Parody stopped coming to his house. He could not judge whether she told Sapna about it, but nothing more abnormal happened.

So much so, Sapna also arranged to have a night stay with him before going to Kolkata, where by she exhibited more than usual enthusiasm.

That night, Sapna said, was her last with him, before the cherished marriage of her younger sister. That night, she took more than her usual quota of drinks and performed a tribal dance to the tune of Punjabi pop. The dance was accompanied by strip tease.

In fact, that night they were not in a hurry, and the nocturnal venture had been planned to include dinner as well.

That Saturday afternoon, Parody had left along with Sapna's husband, as per custom, for a temple about two hundred kilometres away, to be in time early next morning, to offer prayers for the success of her approaching marriage. In their absence that night, Sapna was supposed to attend 'Jagrata' (night long 'kirtan') at the house of one of her employers in the neighbourhood. However, with such a genuine excuse coming her way, she decided in favour of spending the night in sexual bliss with her amorous collaborator, and the programme was chalked out accordingly.

Consequently, Sapna left her house wearing a gaudy dress that evening to go for the 'Jagrata'. She made her presence felt for some time at the 'Jagrata' venue, and soon slipping out went straight to his flat at the pre-fixed hour.

*   *   *

Chapter 29

Kissing and fondling Sapna violently as usual, he did not remove her 'choli' and 'odhni' on arrival that night. Rather, he escorted her lovingly to the dining table, where she gracefully took over the job of pouring drinks. Making a beginning of the nightlong venture, she poured a 'Patiala-peg' for her as well and gulped it down her throat after saying 'cheers', with the same speed as he did. Then with snacks and the second drink in hands, they ventured to the bedroom as usual. In the bedroom, she sat coyly on the sofa by his side, sipping the drink. She did not, however, bother much about snacks. All along, during the fifteen minutes or so they took to finish the second drink, Sapna appeared to be very happy and occasionally he found her shaking her body to the rhythm of pop-music playing on the Channel [V]. Her happiness, she said, resulted from the fact that her younger sister was ultimately going to get married to the good family boy of her choice. So, she said, she had planned the night with him, to celebrate the event in advance.

By the time Sapna went to fetch the third round of drinks she was already 'possessed' by the intoxication. When she sat by his side with the third drink, he casually fondled her shapely thigh and asked if she could dance a strip tease, to which she replied, "Fully well my bull, and may be more than that!" And what he saw next was just befitting his bent of mind.

Curiously enough, Sapna had never played the dancing part before, as she played that night. During the next ten minutes or so, she took to finish the third drink, she became quite intoxicated and consequently more liberated and more desirable.

Punjabi pop singer Daler Mehdy, the heartthrob of millions, appeared on the television with his number 'Ta . . . Ra . . . Ra . . . Ra . . .' when Sapna stood up. Immediately she began shaking her body like a professional. She became faster and faster as the number progressed. Then she took to removing her clothes one by one, beginning with the 'odhni', all in a fast rhythm. It was a prominent tribal dance of her community almost competing with the 'bhangra' of Punjab. After the 'odhni', it was her 'choli', which she took off and threw on his lap like an offering made by a 'chela' to his 'guru'. As she always came without under-garments on such occasions, the removal of 'choli' exposed her shapely and ample bosom, sending waves of passion through his system. Then it was the turn of her 'ghagra' to fall, exposing her whole self. As the pop-song on television neared the end, the dancer-in-the-nude lifted her right leg and moved in circles with speed on her left leg. With the song ending, she finally fell motionless with a thud on to his lap.

The 'dancer' came into form again, with the next number commencing on the small screen after the 'Short break'. This time, it was "Tutak, Tutak, Tutian . . ." of Malkit Singh, another star in the Punjabi pop world at international level. Picking up with the pop-song, the naked beauty made him stand up and took to moving around him, shaking her body perfectly in tune with the ongoing music. That, she told him later was the dance of prosperity, which every woman of her community performed on the eve of her husband's departure to distant lands, to earn livelihood. While dancing around him in a trance like state, she made him discard his 'lungi' as well. Then with every round, she took to bowing before him and touching with both hands, his throbbing male shaft with a sort of reverence. Though he wished to enjoy the situation for some time more, yet the song ended as it should, and both of them fell on to the nearby bed, kissing each other feverishly.

By the time he recovered from the dance, he found himself sprawled on the bed and the naked Sapna with folded legs, sitting atop him. Her inviting thighs were slanted forward, with knees and toes touching the bed on his left and right, and hips resting on his strong thighs. His member in its full form was standing like a bamboo shoot, between her thighs.

Sensing her mood, he placed his hands on her waist in an effort to pull her up and lifting his knees upwards, gave a slant to his thighs. That made her hips slowly slide forward, bringing the parting point of her thighs in touch with his member. Taking a cue, she lifted her hips and slightly bending forward, clutched his shoulders with both hands, giving him a rare view of her hanging breasts. That gave him a sense of closeness with her, and putting his right hand between her thighs, he inserted the head of his maleness into her love-pot. With the real things thus fitting in place and knowing the next steps very well, Sapna moved up and down slowly, with a little help from him, and took the complete rod inside her, ultimately sitting pretty upon his middle.

Then in a lovely tone in that position, she sang a song for him in her own language. The song, she told him, expressed the joy of a damsel under the onslaught of her lover's repeated thrusts during copulation. The damsel in that song said that she wanted neither riches nor fame, and what she wanted were the repeated thrusts of her lover's organ, even if he fixed her on a sand dune.

He also sang a Punjabi song at the occasion, and explained the central idea to her. His song was about a Punjabi boy's massage to his beloved: When I take you, I will take you so hard that you will forget the world around! Well, these are the ways of lovers!

It was about 10pm when they finished with the opening round of lovemaking and after enjoying the resulting bliss, went in for a joint shower. The following hour or so in the bathroom was also equally fulfilling, during which they experienced being one body and mind, under falling water.

Emerging from the bath, they went hand in hand to the dining table, in the nude. Sitting side by side at the table, they poured a 'single' each and began sipping the drink mingled with bouts of cuddling. The dinner ordered on phone and taken in candlelight, added fuel to the fire, further charging them with the energy, sufficient for a prolonged session of lovemaking.

They sat down after the dinner, to watch television. But, being so close and so full of desire, they switched off the television and mounted the bed, with no interference of any kind. It was up and up the golden path, in fits and starts, with his female companion never saying no, until the worshipers in the neighbourhood took to ringing the bells, denoting the conclusion of 'Jagrata' and they fell motionless, in a tight embrace: sleeping.

Getting up after about two hours, they took a hot-and-cold shower, embracing and cuddling. Then taking heavy breakfast, Sapna went home and returned soon for her usual Sunday visit to his home skipping the weekly worship at the main city temple. That was to sleep in his arms in the nude for the better part of that Sunday; fully satisfied with life.

Ah, those were the days!

* * *

Chapter 30

With the time going by as per its never changing speed, the day of departure approached as scheduled and Parody went with her family to the far off Kolkata for her marriage. No doubt, she paid the last customary visit to his house on the eve of departure and accepted from him, the gift of a golden-yellow Punjabi dress, complete with panties set and bra and a small printed towel. The gift also included a golden-yellow pair of high-heel sandals and a purse of the same colour. All this was of course in addition to a sizeable amount of money given to her elder sister, his long-standing lady-love, with the assurance of not asking for repayment.

When the family returned from Kolkata after marriage, Sapna regaled him with the tales of rail journey to Kolkata, and of course the marriage ceremony. From what she told, he could easily calculate that the rail journey to Kolkata commencing in the early afternoon and involving a night stay midway to catch a connecting train at a well-known rail junction, Manmad, took four full nights and the three intervening days in all.

Sapna also spoke very high of the 'goodness' and 'high financial standing' of the family with which her younger sister was 'destined to live a blissful life' under the care of her 'doting parents-in-law' and 'loving husband'. She repeatedly told him that her younger sister had very fondly spoken to her marital family about his affection for her as well. She had also conveyed hand-folded 'Namaskar' to him, along with instructions to take proper care of his 'health and happiness'.

He was still getting hallucinations about Parody, the elusive damsel of his dreams, submitting her virginity to a hitherto unknown person, who, with an overnight marriage ceremony, had got the right to disrobe her, even forcibly as per Indian social norms, when one day Sapna brought news. She informed him that her younger sister had come for the first 'feri' to the parental home after spending twelve full nights with her husband, as per custom. She further told that the husband of the girl accompanying her had since gone back, and that after a 12-night stay, her sister was to undertake the long journey alone to Kolkata by rail on a return ticket. Then with a very sad look she said, "My younger sister is no longer a child and she would certainly reach back safe".

"Why to worry over so trivial a matter?" He asked, and changing the subject, fired another question, "By the way, when does she plan to visit this house?"

"May be soon." She replied with a ruffled look and got busy in house work.

As Sapna took to work, that day and for some days there after, he found she was not in her usual self. During those days, her visits to his house became irregular and brief, and her mood remained so off beat, he could not even dare to broach the subject of Parody's visit to his house. May be, she was merely worried about the return journey of her newly married younger sister. May be, she was preparing herself to bear with the coming separation from her younger sister. May be, her younger sister had ultimately told her of his 'misadventure'. May be, it was something else in her mind. He could not reach any conclusion, but something in her mood told him, something was certainly wrong somewhere, which must have something to do with Parody, and certainly not her journey alone. Was it his hunch or intuition? What would he call it?

Parody came to his house accompanied by Sapna one afternoon, at the fag end of her 'feri'. He had excused himself to slip away from office after lunch that day, on being told by Sapna in the morning about the proposed visit. But, he was shocked to find, there was no force in the hand-folded 'Namaskar' of Parody. Her face was not glowing, as it should after marriage. The only signs of marriage on her were the faded vermilion mark in the parting of her hair and the 'bindi'. He made her sit on an armless chair facing him, while Sapna squatted on the balcony floor by her side. He felt, something was surely amiss, which could have been the cause of Sapna's off beat mood as well.

During the routine exchange of pleasantries, Parody did not exhibit the usual enthusiasm of a newly married girl, to discuss the affairs of her marital family. In the brief discussion, which followed, she just gave a cursory description of the family's real estate business and told him that she would be leaving for Kolkata by train, the next day. To provoke her to speak, he expressed his apology to miss seeing her in bridal dress due to his inability to attend her marriage. She, however, brushed his move aside saying, "I wish, I had not married at all . . ."

Sapna tried to explain by saying that Kolkata being a far away place, "my younger sister will not be able to frequently meet us." But, he for sure felt, that could not be the reason.

"Are you still angry with me?" Parody asked him abruptly, after Sapna left them alone at his instance, to fetch the welcome refreshments from the kitchen across the bedroom and the lobby.

"No, not at all!" He said, adding, "I was rather going to ask the same question to you."

"Would you not give me a farewell dinner, in that case?" She fired the second question after some moments.

"Sure . . . Sure . . . Why not . . . ?" He said, wondering whether she would come alone for the farewell dinner or with her whole family.

"But, I would like to come alone for the dinner." She said, as if sensing his predicament.

However, he pointed out, "It could be considered as improper on your part, to dine with me alone, and go home without escort late night after dinner". So, he suggested, "You can bring your elder sister along for company".

"No! Never on earth . . . ! Never!" She blurted and added after a pause, "I am a married woman now and very much capable of taking decisions of my own . . . My elder sister has in fact done more harm to me than protection, by selecting that rich family groom for me . . ."

She was about to sob saying this, when they heard the footsteps of Sapna. So, suppressing her feelings, Parody changed the subject with a poser to him, whether there could ever be his chance visit to Kolkata, to which he answered in the affirmative. Thus saving the situation, she took to sipping the cold drink and between the sips announced to her sister, she was accepting his invitation for a farewell dinner that evening.

* * *

Chapter 31

After arranging paraphernalia for the 'farewell dinner', he was standing in the balcony, when he saw Parody appear at the street corner and walk with calculated steps, in golden streetlight towards his house, at the given time. She was just like a doll when she first came to his view. She became discernible as his dream-girl, as she came closer, step-by-step.

"It is going to be a memorable farewell!" He told himself and went to the main door to welcome the guest.

When he opened the door, Parody was standing there in full bridal glory. With lowered eyes of a newly married girl and simple smile on her freshly made-up lips, she offered a hand-folded 'Namaskar', and stepping into the house, closed the door behind her, as she had been doing in the past.

Once inside, she stood for a moment in front of him. As he watched wonderstruck, she came closer in a child-like move, and took him in a tight embrace; with her head tucked against his broad chest. Confused at the gust of her affection, he encircled her shoulders with his left arm and secured the door latch with his right hand. Next, taking a few back steps and tenderly pulling her along, he brought her under direct tube light in the lobby. Then making her comfortably stand by him, he caught hold of her chin in a caring gesture.

Obligingly, she lifted her face to see in his eyes. He found her dark unfathomed eyes were moist and a long sigh escaped her quivering lips. May be in a bid to convince her of his affection, he put his right arm also around her shoulders gently pressing her to his body and asked, "What harm has come to you?"

Pressing a sob and remaining in the same clinging position, she said, "I am still a virgin despite spending twelve nights with my husband."

"What do you mean?" He asked, and she said, "It is true!"

Further telling him that her husband had failed to consummate the marriage, due to impotence caused by drug addiction, she asked whether he still loved her and lifted her face further up, as if in an apology for earlier walking over his 'advance'.

Overwhelmed with the momentous feelings, he straightened his body slightly pulling her off the feet, and showered kisses on her done up cheeks, forehead and the chin; wilfully avoiding the lips, partly for fear of transferring the fresh lipstick and partly saving the moment for the time being.

Seemingly enjoying every move on his part, she kept her face in the same inviting position, mumbling something, which perhaps suggested that the lipstick was non-transferable and that he should have gone ahead with the kissing of her lips as well, as the top expression of his love for her.

At the very first look on Parody, he could easily allude that she had taken a lot of care, including a visit to the beauty parlour, for her 'farewell dinner' with him. Her dress consisted of a bright red 'ghagra' with an equally red 'odhni' and a golden-yellow 'choli'. All the three pieces of her dress were embroidered and studded with small mirrors and beads.

She wore traditional gold and silver ornaments, the most prominent being the heavy silver anklets fitted with jingle bells, which created lyrical metallic sounds, when she walked. She was wearing golden-yellow bangles, matching with her 'choli'. Her hands and feet were manicured, and decorated with nail polish, a number of ornamental rings and intricate designs of 'mahendi'. Her golden-yellow and high-heel pair of sandals gifted by him and fully matching with her 'choli', added grace to her walk. She had come with a golden-yellow purse, also gifted by him, hanging from her shoulder.

Parody's 'ghagra' like her elder sister's was secured at the confluence of her waist and the pubic pad; with a colourful and frill-ended cord, knotted on left side. Flowing downward with its numerous folds, he could visualize, the 'ghagra' encompassing her sturdy hips and shapely thighs, giving her the look of a fairy-tale princess, flying on clouds. Her tight 'choli', with its lower fringes much above her belly button, exposed the concave curves of her appealing waist. Also with its plunging neckline, it almost bared the domes of her breasts in the style of Bipasha Basu, while the 'odhni' majestically encased her face, like a fancy photo frame.

Seeing her walk from the street corner towards his house, the thought of her shapely thighs, constantly rubbing against each other, with the legs crisscrossing inside the ample 'ghagra', had sent an electric current down the nerves of the debauchee in him. And by now, he had a fair inkling of what could be in store for him in a short while.

His next move was to offer a cold drink and something sweet to the 'guest' as the customary Indian welcome. However, instead of allowing him to uncork her favourite juice bottle, she took a bite of a 'gulab jamun' and beckoned him to take her on a round of the house, which she said, she had 'tended' for long.

As such, hand in hand they went to all the nooks and corners of the house, including the balcony and the kitchen. Visiting various rooms, she put the curtains in place and arranged the scanty paraphernalia as she had been doing for years. However, unlike other rooms, she paid special attention to the bedroom and the attached bath. Here, besides putting the recently installed rose-colour curtains in place, she replaced the bed sheet and pillow covers with new ones of the matching colour. She also arranged the side table and hung her yellow purse on the wall, perhaps giving a broad hint of her plan to stay overnight. Then she took out from the purse, the small printed towel, gifted by him, and hung it in the bath, where she also checked the working of the shower, giving him a sly look. Thus going through the conducted tour, they returned to the dining table in the lobby, where the packed dinner for two, ordered from a fast-food joint and some other choicest eatables were waiting, to be partaken.

Once again at the table, he tried to open a juice bottle for her. Again, she forbade him from doing so and taunted if he could not offer her "something hard" to drink for farewell.

With such an extra-ordinary demand on her part, he was fumbling for words, when she washed away his confusion, saying, "I am a married woman now, very much responsible for my good or bad . . . I no longer depend upon my elder sister for advice, who has ditched me into this sordid marriage."

Her argument touching the core of his mind, he leapt for the refrigerator, took out two beer bottles, opened one, and poured the contents in two mugs, emptying the bottle in one go. Then he took a bottle of 'Red Knight' whiskey from the nearby cupboard and poured a peg measure each, in the beer mugs, as Punjabi style 'tadka'. And raising the drinks to the good health and happiness of each other, they settled to a farewell drink-n-dine.

As the clamour of the city outside calmed down with the evening changing into night, the successive sips of the 'hard drink' told upon their systems, making them loose the sense of time. They were sitting across the dining table facing each other, when he proffered the first beer mug towards Parody. No body knows how and when they came to sit comfortably on the adjoining chairs. What is worth mention is that forgetting all social taboos and progressing from seemingly unintentional rubbing of sides to holding of hands, they became locked in a perpetual embrace. And, ultimately throwing all cautions to the winds, Parody went over to his lap; an open invitation to him to reconnoitre the tantalizing curves of her stout body, in gay abandon.

Exploring each other for the first time, they were mostly muttering sweet nothings. Occasionally, he helped remove her ornaments; leaving only the noisy silver anklets in place, and she staggered a number of times to the bedroom to place the removed ornaments on the side table.

Astonishingly enough, discussing various stages of their 'matter of fact' relationship of the past many years, Parody tactfully avoided making mention of her recently held marriage and 'over-bossing elder sister'. This was presumably to avoid shaking of salt in the milk of the 'farewell', they were enjoying to the hilt.

Somewhere on the line, Parody also took off her bright red and lavishly embroidered 'odhni' and hung it from a nail on the lobby wall. That exposed her ceremonial 'jalebi-joora', decorated with a string of exuberant jasmine flowers. While fondling her curvaceous body, he undid her 'jalebi-joora', throwing the coconut-smelling cascade of hair over her back, down to her hips. All along expressing his boundless affection for her, he placed the once denied kiss on her face for umpteen times and constantly nibbled at her thin quivering lips. In turn, he provided her with ample opportunity to suck at his tongue, so that she could have an advance feeling of ". . . . the moving parts" of the male and female bodies "fitting together . . ."

The dinner was of Parody's liking. She enjoyed eating, and feeding morsels to him as well with her decorated hands. After the dinner, finished with cold coffee, the scene shifted to the bedroom.

* * *

Chapter 32

Hurriedly he cleared the dining table, and throwing away his formal dress, changed into the easy-to-discard Punjabi 'chadra'.

When he entered the bedroom flexing the muscles of his bare upper body after switching off the no longer required house lights, Parody was emerging from the bath with unsteady steps, and rinsing her hands with the small printed towel she had earlier hung there.

Placing the towel on the pillow side of the bed, she faced the dressing table. Watching herself in the man-size mirror, she converted the cascade of her hair into a hanging knot. Then she switched off the milky tube and put on the red light, giving a dream like tinge to the location. As she staggered past him pretending to be busy in trivialities, he held her by the shoulders and affectionately buried his teeth repeatedly into the left and right sides of her neck. Without hesitation and seemingly flux with anticipation, she clung to him, in a way permitting him to have a free go at her.

They were then standing at the same spot, where Parody had walked on him, about fifteen days before going to Kolkata for her marriage. However, forgetting the ugly event and rather bewitched by the favourable turn of situation, he undid the snap-shut buttons of her 'choli' at the back.

Next, he unhooked the bra and removed the two garments together, exposing the lovely pair of her breasts. With lowered eyes, as if in a reflex action to hide her female charm from his passionate gaze, she embraced him, pressing her bare breasts to his chest.

Encircling her bare shoulders with his left arm, he caressed her shoulder blades with right hand and slowly moved the hand downward, in zigzag movements. Passing the hand over the soft-and-sexy granite back, he fondled her hips for a while and ultimately took the hand to the left side of her narrow waist, resting it on the knot of her 'ghagra' cord.

As he pulled one of the frilled ends of the cord after fumbling with it for a while, the knot gave way and the loose flowing 'ghagra' fell to the carpet below. That exposed her whole self to the vagaries of male onslaught, eternally coveted by the female. Then lifting her face, with his right hand under her chin, he once again planted kisses on her cheeks, forehead and finally the lips; on the sly looking at the trancelike act in the dressing table mirror under red light.

Hugging him in her whole shining and vibrating nakedness, Parody appeared to have fully surrendered; body and mind. Keeping her bosom pressed to his chest, he gently lifted her with a tug of his right hand under her hips and put her flat on the bed. During the act, she somehow discarded her high-heel sandals and took hold of the small printed towel. As he pulled away her 'kachhi' (panties), instinctively, she covered the parting point of her thighs with the towel and intertwined her legs. Her armpits were free from the unwanted hair and so was the pubic area, neat and clean, with inviting body odour. With her applied consent, he placed a pillow wrapped in a towel under her hips, as an aid for the anticipated manoeuvres, and sat for a moment on her side; wondering at the 'opportunity' which had suddenly come calling on him.

While the damsel of his dreams with granite-shining and vibrating body was obligingly lying in the nude, the golden-yellow bangles on her wrists were keeping company with her hands, in a feeble attempt to provide cover to her breasts.

There she was! A nineteen plus married virgin, longing for her initiation into womanhood!

And there he was! A dominating 40-year old bull of a man, ready to take her on the blissful path of copulation!

Well, that was the rare situation, coveted by all men irrespective of caste and creed. And that was the situation, which eludes a majority of men due to a thousand manmade reasons including social norms and taboos in India.

Also, that was the situation, for which countless lovers are known to have sacrificed their precious lives.

To be precise, that was the situation, which Ranjha, the legendry lover of the Punjab of yore, could enjoy only once, when his beloved Heer, since married to one-eyed Saida, went to meet him in an orchard, where Ranjha was camping as a recluse.

That was the situation, which another lover from the Punjab of yore namely Mirza enjoyed only once, and that too at the cost of his life. That was when eloping with his beloved Sahiban on his 'Bukky', Mirza ravished Sahiban in haste under a desert-tree and fell asleep, before both of them were mercilessly slain by the pursuing clan's men of Sahiban.

However watching Parody in the nude, he discarded his 'chadra', lovingly caught hold of her hands exposing the breasts, and shoved himself over to her.

Then, nibbling at her sensual nipples, he sent her into a tizzy, shaking her body from top to toes. As a result, the small printed towel covering the parting point of her thighs fell away, giving him a clear peripheral view of his destination.

Further, planting a caring kiss on her face, he folded his right leg and pressed the knee between her thighs; separating her legs from each other. So, mounting her in the pristine glory of a bull, he adjusted his hip-zone between her parted thighs, and moved his right hand to introduce the adventurous and roughshod head of his male organ, into the coveted slit-like orifice of her love-pot; lubricated with excitement. Doing so, he fondled the clitoris, the most sensitive part of female genitals, which he found was erect with additional blood supply, indicating high state of readiness of the aspiring 'virgin' to receive the 'guest'. Meanwhile, he also felt that the nipples of her breasts had considerably swollen like mushroom-heads, which spoke volumes of her sexual arousal. Then pressing both her hands outwardly on the thick mattress, he made some calculated movements to adjust for 'straight orientation'.

Though the win-win situation for him had since reached the point of no return with Parody already excited enough to play her part, yet he looked into her half-open eyes, with an unspoken request for permission to go ahead with the real part of his tryst with her destiny. His desire to seek her formal nod had suddenly stemmed from realisation of an abnormal difference in their body dimensions.

A cute little 'thing of beauty', as compared to his strong body structure, Parody had various limbs of her body, much smaller than his. So could be, he presumed, the circumference and the depth of her vaginal cavity as compared to the thickness and the length of his throbbing male organ. How could such a small cavity accommodate such a big object without suffering damage? That was a million-rupee question. No doubt, the woman's vaginal cavity, like females of all living creatures on earth, is capable of expanding a lot to facilitate childbirth. But that comes after a plenty of hormonal and other biological changes, which take place inside her body during nine months of pregnancy. What he was dealing with, was a cute little married virgin, and not a woman at childbirth.

Parody had come to him seeking sexual bliss, which her impotent husband could not provide. She must have visualised herself swinging on satisfaction and happiness, following her decision to surrender her virginity to him. What if she suffered undue pain or lasting vaginal injury during copulation with the bull of a man with enormous physical dimensions that he was?

No doubt, she had since seen the enormity of his maleness, pushing between her thighs!

What was required on his part at the occasion? Certainly not brute force, but caution and restraint! So, his aim was to make her fly with him on the wings of sensuality instead of dragging her on the thorny path of lust.

But, during those seconds, heavy with expectation, he found Parody more or less calm and composed. There was no uncontrolled movement of any of her limbs, which could have betrayed an inner conflict or tension. Her breathing was steady and the domes of her breasts were making slow movements up and down, as if waiting to be flattened by the male chest hovering above. There was no effort whatsoever on her part, to make him dismount her. She may be a bit concerned, but certainly not frightened. What could he read in her eyes was, nothing but hope encouraging her to convey yes.

And the 'yes' she very much conveyed, by throwing a flying kiss at him followed by closing of her eyes and turning her face to left; just in readiness to take the 'assault'. If anything, her body language conveyed the eternal female's desire to be physically overwhelmed by her chosen mate.

* * *

Chapter 33

So, with Parody's formal approval and already having found the correct angle, he lovingly forced penetration with small and caring hip-jerks. All the time flattering her with endearments like 'my sweet heart' and 'my brave beauty', he continued the pushing action relentlessly, and ultimately united his rough-and-tough pubic pad, with hers; silken soft.

The process was fraught with danger of injury. The task had to be performed with a lot of care for the cute little married-virgin who had put her faith in him despite many odds. The penetration must have been painful to Parody despite her flared up libido. That was why her stout body was shaking uncontrollably in his firm grip, though there was no attempt on her part to expel the 'intruder' or get herself free with a sudden spurt of force.

That was that, and leaving her hands free, he engulfed her writhing and quivering body in an affectionate embrace, tightly pressing the domes of her breasts to his chest and keeping most of his body weight on his elbows. Parody on her part, clutched his shoulders with both hands and impulsively raising her knees to the maximum, and placed her feet on the backsides of his knees. This perhaps, was to face the pain of the ruptured hymen, mixed with the excitement of first-ever 'entry'. Then, may be relishing the blissful pain, she changed the posture and intertwined her legs with those of him. This way, her shapely legs rising outwardly from left and right of his hip-zone, were twisted inward at the knees and placed in such a way, that her feet were dangling between his legs, as if in a bid to touch each other. The new posture seemed to have given respite to her, as there was no uncontrolled writhing and quivering of her body subsequently, and she offered her thin lips to him for kisses, to which he responded lustily. While kissing Parody in that posture, he had to bend his back upward due to difference of their heights, which in turn released the pressure on her breasts. However, kissing or no kissing, she beckoned him to keep her sturdy breasts pressed to his chest and releasing his shoulders, took to fondling his back lovingly with her tiny hands.

Achieving full entry and keeping his pubic pad in place, he took to deep breathing; feeling the oneness of two longing partners of the sex game.

What a marvellous fete it was on the part of Parody! How wonderfully her vaginal muscles had stretched width wise and lengthwise to accommodate the hefty 'intruder'! Above all, she seemed to be relishing the whole act! Discernible on her face was, a thick layer of happiness, accompanied by her inconsistent muttering of sweet nothings. Could it be a dream, he thought, and pinched his left arm with right hand while keeping Parody's bosom pressed to his chest. The dream it was not, as he very much felt the pinch, and found Parody sensually writhing in his embrace and responding to his lustful manoeuvres.

Parody in the nude, a married virgin, the damsel of his dreams, a fairy in flesh and blood, and Sapna in miniature, was his that night. If there is heaven anywhere, really it was in his bedroom that night! That was the ultimate in physical pleasure and mental satisfaction. The situation sent him into a fit of soul stirring fulfilment. What more could he have asked from life! Virtually nothing more for the time being!

Then in a state of delirious happiness over the favour bestowed upon him by Parody, he took to making up-down movements of his hip-zone. Keeping his legs apart and knees pressed to the bed, he commenced with small withdrawals, followed by caring thrusts. When he found Parody responding rhythmically, he progressively increased the distance between their pubic pads, with every withdrawal followed by a caring thrust. With the pillow underneath helping her meet his thrusts mid-way, Parody closed her eyes in ecstasy and moved her body in tune with him.

Soon, he removed his forearms from underneath Parody's shoulders to gain some leverage for proper thrusts. Parody, then passed her arms through his armpits and took turns in clinging to him in gusts of passion, resulting from his repeated thrusts.

Occasionally, scoring her curvaceous body by taking her naked flesh in squeezing hand-grips from shoulders downward, he placed his hands under her hips, and thus with speedy withdrawals, made vigorous thrusts, which she welcomed with sighs and sensual groans. All along, the jingle bells of her anklets, were keeping company by producing lyrical metallic sounds, with constant movement of her feet, dangling between his legs.

The heat resulting from the fusion of the male and female bodies was so intense, that even in the reasonably cold late October night, beads of sweat constantly appeared on their foreheads. The small printed towel remained handy to wipe out the sweat.

During the bed game, he repeatedly felt sudden movements of Parody's vaginal muscles engulfing his throbbing male shaft. During such moments, she strained her legs inward with full force, abruptly halting his thrusts, and keeping their pubic pads united for long, to enjoy full entry.

She almost burst with excitement, when he placed her legs on his shoulders and applied force at the right place, thus stretching her 'depth' to the maximum with his male shaft. That is the wont of the 'Punjabi' posture, largely coveted by the female of the human species, the world over.

Both of them perhaps wanted to continue the sexual intercourse eternally, when he felt something ready to come out of him. Lo! Warm and dense liquid suddenly broke from his within, through the male shaft, into Parody's reproductive canal. She received semen entering her female receptacle for the first time with rhythmic convulsions of her vaginal muscles, and pleasant hissing sounds.

Those were the moments, when their bodies tended to melt into each other and minds became one, forgetting separate existence, and merging past and future with the present. For some time, as the euphoria of oneness lasted, both of them became motionless, lost into one another, under spell of the resulting bliss. The experience was the fulfilment of a deep-rooted wish, a dream come true, and the culmination of an ardent effort for him. Really!

Parody on her part, appeared to have been transported into the dazzling world of pleasure, from where she did not want to return at all. This was writ large in her half-open eyes and general body language. Alas, the wishes were horses!

As they separated, they found sizeable clots of blood around their genitals, resulting from the rupture of Parody's hymen, which, she dutifully wiped off with the small printed towel. Thus consummating her marriage, they clung to each other in a bid to sleep.

But, the ocean of desire made tidal waves again and again, and by about 4am, when the city rose with the morning walkers thumping on the roads, they had played the game of love four times over, enjoying every move of it.

Parody woke him up by 6am and covering her vital parts with bare hands, beckoned him towards the bath, seemingly to compensate for the abrupt end to his joy of seeing her in the nude, an year back. But, his cup of visual and physical sensuality already full to the brim from the nightlong venture, he changed side and went into a deep slumber, ignoring the rare-in-life invitation.

When Parody offered a cup of tea after finally waking him up by 8am, she was ready to go. She had already had a bath and put on the gaudy bridal dress; with all the ornaments in place, and make-up complete with vermilion mark and 'bindi'. As he was sipping his tea, she fondly folded the small printed towel; accompanying them through the blissful journey, and put it in her yellow purse, presumably to preserve it as a relic.

He accompanied her to the door with his left hand on her back. There was a glow of contentment on her face, when she turned to him across the door, and offered hand-folded 'Namaskar', seeking separation. Then, like a rivulet, cascading on the stony slope of a hill, she went down the stairs, as if dancing to the tune of her anklets. Closing the door, he went to the balcony, and saw her disappear at the street corner into the wilderness of the city, which she was leaving that very day, to join her impotent husband in the distant Kolkata.

* * *

Chapter 34

He treated India as his motherland in real sense, but described it as paradox of a country on the planet earth. Rather than a country he felt more at peace by projecting this vast landmass as a sub-continent within Asia sub-continent. He based his contention on the vastness of India from Siachin in the north to Kanya Kumari in the south, and from Arunachal Pradesh in the east to Gujarat in the west. Further that with 8000 km coastline and about 33,00,000 sq km of area, it is the seventh largest country of the world. It has world's second largest population, which is just over 15% of the total humanity. It has all the four seasons, nicely distributed, and rich variety of flora and fauna.

He was aware that at a point of history, when the humankind the world over lived in aboriginal tribes, this country had 'Harrappa Civilization' from which the modern world has taken the art of town planning. Shipping was developed here about 5000 years back. To create a reservoir for storage of water for irrigation, the first dam of the world was built in the Saurashtra region of this country. Ayurveda developed in this country was the first medical system of the world. The game of Shatranj was invented here. The first university of the world was established at Taxla in this very country, some centuries before Christ, which taught more than 60 subjects to more than 10,000 students. Algebra, trigonometry, and calculus were conceived and developed in this country. This country invented the number system and gave the concept of 'zero' to the world. The decimal system was invented here, 100 years before Christ. Sanskrit, the original language of this country as per Forbes magazine, is the most suitable and easy for use in computer. This country has never attacked any other country in its long history. Until 1896, this country was the only source of diamonds, the world over.

Mark Twain is said to have described this country as a land ". . . . of dreams and romance, of a hundred nations and a hundred tongues, of a thousand religions and two million gods, cradle of human race, birthplace of human speech, mother of history, grand mother of legend, great grand mother of tradition . . ."

This country has a plethora of religions, sub-religions, places and objects of worship including rats, snakes and elephants, dead and alive god-men, ashrams, maths, holy families; all preaching the virtues of honesty, humility, compassion, equality of humankind, certainty of death, futility of greed, respect for elders etc. Every day of the year in this country is associated with this or that religion, religious place, or god-man. Almost all citizens of this country claim to be the followers of this or that religion, religious organization, place of worship or god-man. Yet, in a letter to his mother written on his first visit to this country, Winston Churchill described it as ". . . . a God-less land of snobs and bores."

In fact this country used to be a geographical region with many independent kingdoms, all perpetually trying to subjugate each other. That was until Islamic invaders humbled the warring kingdoms followed by the British colonial rule. The country achieved freedom in 1947 after a prolonged struggle and ushered into an era of democratic rule. Its army and civil bureaucracy are among the largest in the world. It is a nuclear power launching satellites with plans to send spaceships to the moon. Its engineers said to be the mind power of the world are developing fifth-generation fighter aircrafts.

But, he felt to his chagrin, that the most obnoxious aspect of governance in this biggest democracy of the world is the criminal-politician-bureaucrat nexus, about which less said the better. The result of this unholy nexus is all pervading corruption and double standards in public and private life. Things are so topsy-turvy in this country that politicians are the most unethical and unprincipled players of governance: those in power and those in the opposition. While most of the ruling politicians irrespective of their party(s) remain busy in devising ways and means to amass wealth and the subsequent damage control exercises besides enacting impracticable laws, those in opposition have no motive other than blocking the government business in Parliament and the State Assemblies. No wonder the progress is a casualty here and even well into the 21st century, seventy out of a hundred persons have to live off agriculture here which has only the fifth of country's total income. Furthermore, the constitution of the country swears by secularism, but all political parties exploit religious sentiments of the people to the maximum to get votes. So much so, the communists theoretically opposed to the concept of religion also unashamedly participate in religious practices like this and that 'pooja' in this country, just for the sake of votes. How nicely the tail piece of Khushwant Singh's column in a respectable daily describes the situation! "Do not worry about those who have come through boats. Our forces can easily defeat them. Worry about those who have come through votes. They are our real enemies."

He often lamented in his heart of hearts about the general public of India being tragically forgetful, so as to elect the same sets of unprincipled politicians and even known criminals again and again. No doubt, of late the country's judiciary at the higher levels and the Election commission have taken up measures aimed at cleansing the polity, but ever increasing population, illiteracy and religion/caste based divisions are the main hurdles.

Next to the self-aggrandizing politicians, he despised the government employees, who flout the rules and misuse their official position to make money. Most of them come late, shirk work on various pretexts, enjoy atrociously extended lunch break, and leave for home early on routine basis, as a matter of right. That is despite the fact that they are entitled to about 200 holidays in a year. Also despite the fact that a very big chunk of them gets jobs and promotions under vote-bank policies, even being low on merit and very poor in performance. To behave in such a shameless manner, the employees are helped by numerous trade unions, whose main aim is to ensure pay and perks for them without doing any work.

Another slur, he loathed: nothing happens in this country without 'sifarish' or bribe. If you want a ration card, a passport, or a driving licence. If you want a correction in your inflated power or telephone bill. If you want railway reservation. If you want to register the sale or purchase of property. If you want to admit your child in a school of your choice. If you want timely admission and doctor's attention in a government hospital. Cent per cent chances are; you will have to pull strings from 'above' through 'sifarish', or cough up the befitting bribe.

In this country, the human rights organizations are only concerned about (read against) the killing of terrorists and criminals by the security forces, while they have nothing to say about (against) the killing of innocent and unarmed people including women and children by the terrorists and criminals. In this country, the police have become an instrument of suppression in the rulers' hands. A prime minister swearing by democracy, whose election was invalidated by the court for using unfair means, had the tenacity to remain in power by imposing 'emergency'. In this country, the security guards including a favoured one killed a prime minister.

In this biggest democracy of the world, 'leaders' are only born in certain families. Some of this country's natural citizens are loyal to a neighbouring country to the extent that they do not even tolerate the victory of this country over that country on the playground. A number of this country's citizens still take out umbrellas when clouds appear in Moscow or Beijing.

A big majority of the motorists including those holding valid driving licences in this country do not have the basic knowledge (read sense) of traffic rules, besides being foolish enough so as not to recognise the rights of other road users. Most of them stop at the red light crossing only when the police are present. Besides, most of them are totally unaware of the purpose of 'zebra crossings'.

In this country people throw garbage on public places, relish in extending their houses/shops etc on to the roads and streets, steal power with impunity, try to break the queue where ever possible, kill each other in the name of religion, get jobs on the force of fake degrees or bribe, and conduct pre-birth tests to abort baby girls.

In this country, industrialists, traders, vendors, shopkeepers, transporters, private practitioners, and various types of other self-employed people seem to be thriving on mere evasion of taxes. The moment the government attempts to streamline the tax structure, they raise an outcry.

In this country god-men live like kings. The defence forces are short of thousands of officers while countless educated boys and girls face unemployment. The lawyers and court officials fleece the harried people seeking 'justice' from the court. The pending court cases go on piling up resulting in agonising delay in dispensing of justice while a good number of judges' posts perpetually remain vacant. Some people even born about or after the freedom-year (1947) get pension as 'freedom fighters' while there are many instances of real freedom fighters facing disease and starvation in old age.

In this country, drought, death and diseases are attributed to the 'anger' of this or that deity. Industrialists take huge bank loans and refuse to pay back under various pretexts. Some persons manufacture synthetic milk using chemicals like urea to mint money. Chemicals potentially harmful to human health are used for growth and preservation of vegetables, fruits etc. for easy money. Those accused of corruption and other malpractices move about in the society without an iota of guilt on their faces. The list is long! So much so, even those engaged in managing the affairs of various religions and religious places seem to believe that being religious and using dubious means to make a livelihood are two different things.

This country has three names: India, Bharat, and Hindustan, all officially valid. No short of a paradox! Yes or no?

* * *

Chapter 35

He was at the tail end of a long winding queue of harassed looking men and women in front of a railway ticket-window. There was a rush of activity all around. Hefty policemen flaunting their batons in the air to bring home their authority to the lesser mortals. Red-shirted coolies running relentlessly with pieces of luggage precariously balanced on their heads. Fearful and weepy children grudgingly trailing their commanding mothers. Vendors raising pitched voices to announce their wares including creaky toys, stale biscuits, tasteless tea and 'pakoras', export-rejected under garments, and duplicate cold drinks. The long-distance train was about to arrive any moment. Yet the long winding queue ahead of him was just not moving. That, because the cantankerous 'babu' behind the window was wasting time in gossip with those who were approaching him out of the queue on the force of familiarity or 'sifarish' for tickets. He was also sipping tea from a dirty cup.

Parody, with whom he had decided to elope to some distant land, was hiding behind the police post to avoid being caught. Soon the train thundered in, and with the people jostling to get in, the platform became a boiling pot. All those standing in the queue rushed to board the train without bothering for tickets. As part of the hysterical crowd, he boarded the train and managed to occupy two seats. But by that time there was no trace of Parody, and leaving his briefcase on the seat, he rushed out to search for her. He looked for her all over the platform, under the huge circus tent symbolizing the waiting hall and at the tea-stalls. But, she was nowhere to be seen.

Suddenly the train chugged out taking his brief case. He ran helter-skelter, panting for breath but full of hope. Soon he saw a motley crowd surrounding a wrestling ring on the bank of a vast river. In that ring, he spotted Parody dancing in an orange-colour sleeveless frock. Her bare legs thriving to the tune of a pop song and the hair done in a knot atop her head were just fascinating. In the whirlwind of her self circling movements, her frock often got lifted above hip level exposing her red 'kachhi'. As he tried to make his presence felt to her, he found her climbing a slanting coconut tree with great speed like a squirrel. From the tree, she jumped on to a running horse and sped away gesturing with her hand for him to follow. As he ran bare-foot to catch up with the horse, he found himself held up in a traffic jam and heard a familiar honking with fits and starts. That in fact was the ringing of his doorbell.

Well, that was his sweet-and-sour dream around late forenoon following the blissful night with Parody. Sapna broke the dream, with repeated ringing of the doorbell, and he staggered as if in a trance to the main door. Ushering her in, he just speculated about the possible reason of her visit. May be, she had come to ask for some money, he thought, and assessed with his mind's eye, the amount he could part with. But that was not the reason.

The mystery cleared up when Sapna narrated non-stop, for what she had come: "I wonder how you would react, but my younger sister wants you to accompany her to Kolkata. That is mainly, because I do not want her to undertake the four-night journey alone. Is it not dangerous for a newly married girl to venture on such a long journey without escort? You know, she has to change the train as well on the way, involving a night stay at the busy Manmad junction. What if she faces some problem? The world is so full of tricksters! Anything can happen! I am afraid!"

"Why do you worry at all? I can do anything for you! When dose the train leave?" He blurted in one go without thinking twice.

"Is it that easy? The train leaves by 3pm. What about your leave and railway reservation?" She asked, somewhat astonished at his favourable response.

"Why bother? You go and tell her to be ready by 2pm sharp." He almost ordered her, and she darted.

There were three hours plus left to the train's departure and he acted in haste to arrange emergency leave with a telephonic request to his boss. Then he withdrew sufficient cash from his saving account in the ICICI Bank, which was functioning on holiday, thanks to the policy of liberalisation, reluctantly adopted by the powers that be in India.

While he was busy in hurried preparations, his mind made a plan, which unfolded during the coming days, exactly as he wanted. Certainly, Deepak Chopra, the US-based Indian 'thinker' is absolutely correct in his 'Practical guide to the fulfilment of your dreams', where he asserts that "Left to itself with a positive idea, the human mind is a great schemer".

"Where are you taking me? The train is due to arrive merely in fifty minutes or so". Parody bedecked in a colourful bridal-suit asked, a bit perplexed, when the taxi took a deserted but well maintained road outside the city, instead of heading for the railway station.

"To Kolkata of course!" He said, in a reassuring tone.

"I don't suspect your intentions, but this is not the way to railway station."

"You are right, no doubt. But, we are going to Kolkata by air."

"But, the railway journey takes four nights to Kolkata. So they would be expecting me, only on the day due as per my return ticket."

"What if we reach today evening itself?"

"But, the journey by rail could have kept us together for four long nights and the intervening days. Uninterrupted at that. Yes, why not?"

"But my dear little doll, who stops us from peacefully staying at a hotel in Kolkata, instead of shuttling by railway trains till the stipulated day for you to reach back?"

"O, I see!" Parody exclaimed and calmed down as the taxi approached the airport.

The flight to Kolkata was eventless but for some excited questions asked by Parody travelling by air for the first time, before both of them were overtaken by sound sleep.

The five-star City Hotel near Kolkata Airport where they checked in after landing had an aura of elegance about it, the like of which Parody had never experienced before.

Per chance, the hotel was through its Silver Jubilee Celebrations those days, and was lavishly done up for the event. Naturally, the hotel staff was in celebration mode and over-courteous. The 'goree-chittee' receptionist was a well-proportioned girl of about 22 years. He booked a suite on the top floor with a spacious balcony. The bewitching receptionist took special pains to flaunt the names of some VIP guests, who she claimed, had stayed in that suite.

"What an unpolluted beauty! Hi . . . Hi! What do you say?" The receptionist remarked with a flash of mischievous grin, when he mentioned the identity of Parody in the hotel register as his Personal Secretary.

"Thanks. How nice to find beauty praising beauty!" He remarked closing the register.

"Have a nice stay! Very lucky to have a thoughtful boss! Hi . . . Hi! What do you say?" The receptionist said, and patted the back of Parody after handing over the key to him.

Having spent her life so far doing domestic jobs for ever-complaining middle-class wives, Parody was just wonder-struck over the attention paid to them by the receptionist, and later the usher who escorted them to their suite. She was also amazed at the lavish tip he gave to the usher.

"Have you earlier been to this place?" Parody asked, may be unable to hide her curiosity, after they were left alone in the tastefully furnished suite.

"No. Never. I have only been reading about Kolkata in books and news papers." He told her.

"But, the way these people are treating us and the familiarity they are exuding, certainly makes me wonder!"

"That is their job my love! By the way, what about some familiarity between you and me, now that we are alone?"

And before she could say anything, he took Parody in a bear hug. Extremely happy over the favourable turn of events, she was more than willing. So, after some love-soaked hugging mixed with passionate turns and twists on the majestic bed, they seemed to be heading for a round of the sex game. Accordingly, he undid the string knot of her 'ghagra' and kissing her feverishly, took to fumbling with her 'kachhi'.

But that was not to be, as there was a knock on the door followed by ringing of the musical bell. Tingling . . . lingling . . . Tingling . . . lingling! With this, in a perplexed move, Parody darted to the dressing cabin, clutching her 'ghagra', while sorting out his ruffled clothes, he cautiously opened the door for the visitor.

What he found at the door was nothing but anti-climax: a bearer carrying the evening coffee!

Also there was an invitation card for a 'care-free evening of drink-dance-and-dine', as part of Silver Jubilee Celebrations of the hotel.

Coffee finished, he took Parody to the hotel's boutique to convert her into a mod-mod Personal Secretary, because, somehow it had dawned upon him, her appearance in that gaudy bridal-dress did not merge well with the hotel crowd, and attracted unwanted public attention.

"Yes sir! Here I am in my new 'Avatar'!" Parody said joining him after an hour in their suite, where he was waiting. In accordance with his instructions, the boutique girls had slipped Parody into a knee-length frock of orange colour, without sleeves and with plunging neckline. Her hair was done up in a tight knot atop her head, slightly adding to her height. The 'bindi' and mangal-sutra were gone. All that with her fancy pair of dancing shoes, single-strip necklace and matching ear-tops, gave her a real girlish look. It was already late evening by then and the bewitching receptionist flashed another mischievous grin, as they passed by her, hand-in-hand, towards the Dining Plaza of the hotel, for the 'care-free' evening.

The Dining Plaza was a semi-circular hall, sufficient to seat about three hundred guests. It was adequately lit and furnished, befitting the celebrations. The entry took them to the side of a dancing-floor commanded by a rostrum. The hall was lined with dining tables of various sizes, placed at respectable distance from each other. Smartly dressed bearers were shuttling here and there with loaded trays.

The air was filled with lovely pop, as well as the pleasing aroma of free-flowing liquors. About two hundred guests of all ages were enjoying the courtesy of the hotel. They were a decent crowd of males and females: young and not so young, old and not so old, thin and not so thin, fat and not so fat. There were whole families, newly-married-couples, free-lancers, and of course some loners. While the dancing-floor was alive with some male and female bodies shaking to the rhythmic tunes of pop-music, some guests were watching intently from their seats and some others were engrossed in gossip.

On entry, they were received by an over-courteous usher and taken to a table of their choice by the side of the dancing-floor, where they sat side by side. Parody surveyed the scene with astonishment while he ordered drinks with a fat tip to the bearer to ensure good service. Scanning the people's faces, Parody perhaps tried to find out if some curious pair of eyes could be prying at them.

But, she found none who could be interested in them and so she exclaimed, "What a heavenly place! We are in a crowd and yet alone! No prying eyes! No wry faces! No malice! No cat calls! Nothing of the sort! Only love, love, and love, all around! Where have you brought me? Who are all these people? Do they really exist on earth? Is this the real world? Could it be my hallucination? Could it be just a dream? I fail to understand! Really! Yes, why not?"

The drinks arrived soon and with "cheers" for each other's health and happiness, they took a double sip each and became a part of the marry-making crowd of faceless people.

* * *

Chapter 36

Parody was almost in stupor, when he 'carried' her to their suite from the party by mid-night. By that time, the bewitching receptionist had gone off duty and they were saved from her mischievous grin. Despite becoming moderately drunk half way through the party, amazingly enough Parody had given almost non-stop dance performances. The situation had resulted from a dance competition among the female guests organised by the hotel management. The purpose of the competition was to select a 'Dancing Doll' whose photograph was to adorn the hotel lobby. In fact, Parody was reluctant to participate in the dance competition and it was only at his insistence that she agreed. By the time the competition was announced, they were already through two rounds of Red Label Scotch and had resolved to go in for an early dinner after one more round, obviously to plunge in the game of love as early as possible.

When the announcement came, they had just lifted the scotch-on-the-rocks and he asked Parody if she could participate in the dance competition. With a sip at the drink, she replied in negative and nudged him to order the dinner. Actually, he was also in a hurry to take her to bed and did not want to waste any more time. But, intuition told him to press the proposal with the hope of something more favourable. So, without caring for her refusal, he signalled her 'entry' to the announcer and caressed her back prompting her to join the competition.

The miracle happened, and without wasting any time, Parody gulped the drink in hand and leapt to the dancing-floor. The competition consisted of a 20-minute performance by a dozen unnamed participants, to the changing pop-tunes on the orchestra, while the judges were to select the winner. The performance commenced with a bang under glaring lights; all eyes looking at the pretty dancers, and cameras whirring and flashing relentlessly. As the dance progressed, about half of the participants opted out. But, Parody remained steadfast and flawless. Her steps continued to be rhythmic and fascinating all along. The swaying of her hips and tossing of braless breasts could be described as nothing but just bewitching. The tight knot of hair atop her head and her knee-length frock of orange colour gave her the appearance of a 'Dancing Doll' for real. As the dance went on and on, all eyes became focussed on Parody and the clapping hands began to accompany her movements in unison.

With what he was looking at in astonishment, the selection of Parody as 'Dancing Doll' appeared to be the foregone result. And that was what happened when the judges gave their verdict! Hurrah!

As the selection was announced with a thunderous applause, Parody was taken to the rostrum, where the chief-guest honoured her with a crown and an offer of free stay for two in the hotel's VIP Suite for five nights. The only string tied to the offer was that the 'Dancing Doll' was to give a dance performance every evening during the five-night stay in the hotel. However, for that she was to be 'paid' per evening in addition to the shower of cash from the guests if any.

The crowning ceremony over, Parody trembling with happiness over her success came straight to him with open arms. On his part, he took her in a tight embrace and kissed her hard in full public gaze with cameras flashing. Sitting thereafter for another round of scotch, already ordered by him in celebration, he thought, that was the time to order the dinner.

However that was not, because, Parody was requested by the announcer to give a 5-minute solo performance on the dancing-floor.

The solo finished with all eyes glued to the action, followed by a shower of currency notes in praise. Then there was a request from the guests for another solo. Then another. And then another.

Anyhow, Parody did not refuse even once, as she was in a mood to oblige every body. Moreover, there was that shower of cash as encouragement!

One more round of scotch was taken by Parody in between the dances and he took two. By the time the dinner was served, she was fully 'possessed' by the alcoholic drinks, and there was no way out for him, but to almost 'carry' her to their suit all the way from the Dining Plaza.

Parody had given a fascinating show of hip swinging and body shaking that evening. By showing her charms on the dancing-floor in an uninhibited manner and winning the 'Dancing Doll' competition, she had certainly made him proud as her escort, and a target of many envious glances, giving him an inflated ego. Into the bedchamber at mid-night with the obliging and intoxicated damsel of his dreams, it was all win-win situation for him. Well, by that time, his senses too were almost out of control from boozing. So disrobing Parody, he fell upon his dream girl in a twilight state of mind, and it was only next day when she affectionately showed his teeth marks on her breasts, shoulders, thighs etc. that he could judge, what he had done to her.

The next day was just hilarious. After enjoying the swing of circumstances during night, they got up late. The first thing they did on getting up was the counting of cash showered by the admiring guests on Parody at the dancing-floor. They ordered brunch after joint-bath with the idea of having an undisturbed day, to catch up with sleep, so as to enjoy the coming night.

The VIP Suite to which they were made to shift after the brunch was just marvellous. The coming night was the first of their five-night free stay, as per Parody's entitlement. What a princely treatment! Spending time in that situation, they had nothing particular to do except love chatting and sleeping in an embrace until evening when Parody was taken away for make-up before appearance at the dancing-floor.

Parody called him to the make-up cabin, near the dancing-floor, some time before her appearance, and asked him to order drinks, which she said she required to shun inhibition.

Her appearance in full make-up and a mini dress was just magnificent. Immediately after three stints of solo dancing, she beckoned him to lead her to their suite where she had ordered the dinner sans drinks through room service. How nice of her!

Soon after the dinner, he thought it was time for what they were staying there and took Parody to the waiting bed. There was no difficulty in removing her dancing gear, and mounting her in the glory of a bull. The to-and-fro movements of copulation were just in the rhythm of the pop-song to which Parody had danced only a short while ago.

Warranted by the exigencies of passion, the 'four-night journey' of Parody to Kolkata was extended to six nights, which gave them seven-night 'togetherness' in all. That was more than 50% of the customary twelve nights. Not a bad planning! Yes! Where there is will, there is a way!

The cover up? You mean for the additional two nights taken in 'reaching' Kolkata? That came easily! Yes, that was arranged with Parody making telephone calls to her in-laws, in a harassed voice, supposedly from wayside railway stations, to inform about 'late-running' of the first train and the consequent 'missing' of the other.

The late running of trains? That is every day happening and very much plausible in India, where the corrupt and lethargic political system allows the government servants to have the cake and eat it, and that too at leisure and as per their sweet will. Proof? What proof? Such things are synonymous with our paradox of a country: India, Bharat, Hindustan.

* * *

Chapter 37

About two months after his return from Kolkata, his punishment posting ended with promotion and transfer to his home state: Punjab. So, spending a thanks-giving night with Sapna, and showering her with parting gifts, including lasting bites on her breasts, at her insistence under a heavy doze of whisky, he bid farewell to that 'City of joy'.

However, the haunting memories of Sapna and Parody forced him to remain in touch with them. In due course, Parody informed him of a son born to her, whom she described, as the luscious fruit of her 'weeklong congress of flesh and spirit' with him. Further, within a few months she told him that her parents-in-law and the drug-addicted husband had passed away one by one and her childless 'jeth' had taken her as second wife, giving her full control of the family's real estate business. With the passage of time, she took to moving about in an air-conditioned car. Also following the death of her crippled mother, she shifted Sapna along with her husband to Kolkata. One thing, which she often mentioned in her telephonic conversations with him was, her longing to be with him. How earnestly she wished to repeat their nostalgic odyssey-in-secrecy, even if only once!

Sapna too went on prodding him to visit them. Often calling him from the secrecy of PCO cabins, she imitated the sensual noises and sweet nothings to remind him, of their gone by days of sexual bliss. Also very affectionately, she often pleaded, he should see for himself the turn for better, taken by the life because of her and her younger sister's resolve to struggle against odds as per his 'advice'.

At last, the flames of intense desire and hope burning in their minds, created an opportunity for him after about four years, to fly to Kolkata on an official tour in late May. The 5-day conference, which he was to attend, consisted of only 2-hour sessions in the forenoon, with afternoon free every day. Thus, landing at Kolkata on a Sunday evening, his conference got going on Monday, which was scheduled to conclude on Friday, with the weekend left free.

He could not recognise Parody at first look in the hotel lobby, where she had been waiting for him, when he returned after the opening session of the conference, well before lunch. The meeting was pre-planned, and he was looking for a 'sari'-clad woman of orthodox type, supporting a big 'bindi' on forehead and heavy doze of vermilion in the parting of hair.

What he found instead was, a cell-phone wielding, mod-mod butterfly, in a pair of jeans with a see-through sleeveless T-shirt, and supporting a pair of Ray Ban goggles. With her shoulder-length hairstyle and a heavy purse, she wore a sparkling 6-piece diamond-set. A well-dressed maidservant was in tow, in control of her son. Searching for the familiar face of his 'orthodox ladylove' in the lobby crowd of the five-star hotel, he looked at his watch, and took a seat with an eye on the entrance. But, already present in the hotel lobby, she appeared from nowhere before him, and proffered a hand to shake in a suave manner, with a lovely "Hello!" There she was! His Parody in a new 'avatar'! How comic!

Sitting in the lobby for about ten minutes, Parody exchanged formal pleasantries with him. She also introduced to him, her naughty son, Babloo, a chip off the block that he was. But, unaware of his real relationship with him, and unfamiliar with the likes of him, the boy evinced no interest in him, and shied away to the lap of his beautiful keeper. So, wasting no time, Parody packed the child back to home along with the maid in a taxi, and both of them zoomed by lift, to his 20th floor hotel room, where he had arranged a lunch-for two, through the 'Room Service'.

Once in the room, Parody threw away her heavy purse and the cell-phone, and held him in a tight embrace. Together, they fell on the bed, and took to kissing and cuddling, without uttering a single word. Then, recovering from the ecstasy of the cherished meeting, they went to the sofa, and poured beer in celebration. Finishing a beer bottle with speed and holding each other, they were compelled by libido, to discard their clothing.

Again to the bed, they became one, with his hips making steady up-down movements, and both of them making eternal sensual noises. The climax came in due course for both, and they remained motionless for some time, forgetting the world outside.

Ultimately returning to a bit of normalcy, they realised, there was still an hour and a half to lunch, and so they went in for a shower.

Under the shower, with Parody in the nude in his arms, his mind raced back and prompted him to ask the nagging question.

"I have something to ask you." He said with a bite on her cheek.

"Carry on." She said, moving her hands on his back.

"You knew I loved you so much. Why did you run away when I kissed you some days before your marriage?"

"Yes I did. There was a solid reason." Her response was prompt.

"Tell me that." He said, with another bite.

"No. Not now. May be, I would like to tell you only when I go to see you off at the airport. For now, I simply want to be one with you."

"Sure?" He asked, and sitting on the stool under the shower, beckoned her to his lap, wondering what could be her answer.

"Sure!" She said, and sitting on his thighs with parted legs dangling on both sides, she put the garland of her arms around his neck. So, with Parody's corpulent breasts rubbing against his chest, the water melting over their bodies and falling on the marble floor began to make metallic sounds like muffled jingle-bells.

Holding Parody in the nude, with the shower automatically changing from cold to hot and vice versa, he felt his spirits going up and up. His joy knew no bounds, when she affectionately applied liquid-soap to his body, playing with the foam, all the while. It was long time back, when he had held her so in the City Hotel near Kolkata Airport. It was long time back, when he used to have joint-showers with her elder sister, his longstanding partner-in-sex. It was long time back, when he had the chance to enjoy the company of Rachni and Dolly, his wives of convenience. But, all that was lost to the 'past', while Parody was a thing of the 'present'. Moreover, 'variety is the spice of life' they say, and so was his Parody. A variety! What a beauty she was, and how much enamoured she was to him!

Holding Parody in the nude under shower, he was immersed in his chain of thoughts, when she pinched his arm and asked, "How much time can you spare for me? Can you overstay your weeklong tour? I want to get lost somewhere along with you for some time. May be I want to have an extended honeymoon with you. May be, I wish to have one more chip off your block."

"Done!" He said, adding, "I'll take long leave to be with you," and asked, "By the way, when did you have the last 'puncture'?"

"Ended yesterday only. So you agree?"

"What about your 'jeth'-turned-husband?"

"Leave that to me. No hindrance. I will manage. I have already sent him to a nature-cure hospital near Darjeeling, where I often go by air to see him. And no problem with money too. I want you at any cost."

"How would you justify the pregnancy, resulting from your stay with me, in that case?"

"No problem! For that matter, I will have my 'extended honeymoon' with you in a hotel near Darjeeling, and once or twice sleep with my husband as well, in the nature-cure hospital, where he has a separate room to himself. That way, the pregnancy would be attributed to him, and especially so to the so-called improvement in his maleness resulting from the therapy he is taking. Yes, why not? Any doubt?"

"What about your elder sister and her husband? Are they not living with you? I want to meet them any way?"

"They are no problem too. They live comfortably in a good house at the other end of the city. 'Jijaji' is no more a drunkard. We have since got him cured of addiction to liquor. He works in a security agency with good salary. My sister works in a beauty parlour of repute, run by a Japanese woman. But she remembers you too much. Especially for your sermons to face the life courageously. I will send her here some day. But, no hurry! She does not know of your arrival yet."

"O, I see." He remarked, and took Parody to the bathtub, where they frolicked in water for some time, before putting on easy wear for the 'Room Service' to arrive with lunch.

Taking a 'Patiala-peg' each of Vodka followed by a light lunch, they watched television for about three quarters of an hour. And with sensuality taking the better of them, it was over to the bed again, for a game of love: carefree! Through with it, the sleep took over, and by the time he woke up, there was no trace of Parody, but for her hand-written note: Same time tomorrow. Yours forever in the nude under shower and with love!

* * *

Chapter 38

Next day was like any other day with only one difference. A big one at that. Parody did not turn up at the given time. Skipping the lunch after a long and anxious wait, he tried to sleep, but without success. Repeated calls on her cell phone met with 'no reply', while her home number repeated her taped version, 'I am out. Please record your message if any'.

What could be the reason? She was so anxious to be with him. The thought kept nagging him all the while. He planned to go out to pass time, but every time he thought of going out, something from within stopped him in his heels. Lest she comes in his absence, he thought every time he stood up to go out, and decided to wait for her in his room itself.

Passing the afternoon and the evening in anxious wait for Parody, he finished his dinner. There after he sat before television, still waiting for the miracle to happen, though the hope had almost dwindled to point of no return. Sitting, he recapitulated the earnest, with which she had been pressing him all along, to visit Kolkata. But, she would fail him even on the very second day, despite making sincere promise, was just beyond his comprehension. Immersed in such thoughts, he looked at the watch, to find to his dismay, the time was 9.45pm. That, he concluded, could be too unearthly an hour for a single woman to venture out of home in Kolkata, and so he decided to go to bed. Still the intuition told him to wait until 10pm, before saying die, and he took a chair again to sit; waiting.

And the miracle did happen, because just at the dot of the deadline fixed by him, there was a familiar knock on the door.

Parody was moderately drunk when she entered, profusely apologizing. Anyhow, ignoring what she said, he just lifted her bodily, and laid her on the bed: kissing all over her face and crushing her under his weight.

"This is for what I have been longing all along!" She said when he released her from his grip.

"Do you know how madly I was waiting for you today?" He asked, still anxious to kiss her.

"Would you like to know the reason?"

"I don't care, now that you have come."

"What about your dinner? I have already taken my fill."

"I told you, I don't care."

"Why delay then? An early bird catches the worm, they say. My explanation can certainly wait. By the way, do you know, I am staying overnight, to sleep carelessly in your arms?" She said in one go, may be to sooth his nerves, and stood before him as if asking him to unzip her blue jeans.

Placing a pillow under her hips, and uniting his pubic pad with hers denoting full entry, however, he desisted from commencing the up-down motion of his hip-zone, and asked, "May I know the reason now?"

"Here you are! How apt!" She remarked, and clutched his thighs comfortably with her legs.

So, with his proverbial finger on trigger, Parody told him, she was busy in a real estate deal for whole day, whereby she had made fifty thousand rupees in commission. And that, later she had to go to the women's club, for a pre-planned engagement.

"Very convincing and business like!" He remarked after listening to her, and added, "I am really happy to see your transformation."

"You see the life comes only once. Why to take it lying down? These are your words. I distinctly remember, you had been telling my elder sister. Yes, why not?"

"Very brave of you! I am proud and surprised! How could you do all this?"

"Well, it's a long story. Are you prepared to listen?"

"I would love to . . . ." He said, adjusting his body weight on his elbows, but keeping the pressure of his pubic pad over hers.

"Every thing was so-so, till your son was born to me, and my parents-in-law and husband passed away, one by one. Then the things moved with speed. My childless 'jeth' being a weakling, his in-laws had an eye on our family riches, and so they tried to oust me from the house. To begin with, they tried to tarnish my image, by accusing me and my son, of being ill-omened and responsible for the deaths in the family. Having learnt from you, of all such things being absurd and product of clever minds, I decided not to take the things lying down, and acted in haste. So, I chalked out a plan and sprang into action. As my first move, I created a situation for my childless 'jeth' to take me as his second wife."

"So intelligent of you! How could you do that?" He asked, with a kiss on her lips, and making her feel his male shaft inside her, with a tug of his hip-zone.

"Yes, I could do that very easily and without an iota of guilty conscience." Parody said, adding, "Believe me. In fact, it was all due to your sermons heard in my teens, which I didn't believe then."

"But I am impatient to know how your 'jeth' took you as his second wife."

"No problem! For that, I took to serving my 'jeth' and 'jethani' obediently; taking full care of cooking, cleaning, washing etc. in the house. In the process, I encouraged the 'jeth' to spend his evenings at home. This I did in a comic way. As the 'jeth' exchanged hot words with his wife one evening in an excuse to go out for boozing, I appeared on the scene with folded hands in my usual 'ghungat'. Then taking the 'jeth' to the drawing room by request, I made him sit on the sofa and asked him to wait for a moment. Waiting nonplussed, he was bewildered to see me return and place before him, a liquour bottle of his choice along with a glass, ice-cubes and fish cutlets. By that time the 'jethani' had also barged in, but not caring for her, I poured a heavy peg 'on the rocks' and beckoned the 'jeth' to lift the glass. As he obeyed, I got hold of the protesting 'jethani' by the arm, and took her out of the drawing room, almost by force. When I returned to the drawing room after about five minutes, the 'jeth' had already finished the heavy peg poured by me, and was munching the fish cutlet tastefully. Without uttering a word, I poured one more 'on the rocks' and serving a fish cutlet again went out to console the cursing 'jethani'. By the time the 'jeth' finished with the fourth 'on the rocks' to the assortment of heavy fish cutlets, he became 'possessed' with heady liquour, and forgetting the dinner, went to his bedroom for a sound sleep. From that evening onward, I took to serving drinks to the 'jeth' regularly, despite stiff opposition from the 'jethani'. More often than not, I kept hovering about him every evening, pouring drinks for him and speaking to him in hushed tones.

With all that going on for about a week, the 'jeth' not only took to praising my figure, but also became bold enough to caress my thigh one day, for amorous reason. That was precisely what I wanted, but outwardly refusing to oblige, I pushed his hand away with a jerk and the hushed remarks, "No, no I'm not of that type . . . and what if your wife finds it?"

However, during the days to come, I kept the 'secret' and continued arousing curiosity of the 'jeth' in me. For that matter, I also took to wearing tight dresses in the evenings so as to expose my body curves from close range while serving drinks to him.

Soon one day, when I found the 'jeth' doting on me under intense intoxication, I sat by his side lifting my 'ghungat' for a moment, but still refused to let him go any further. As he became restless to become intimate with me in the coming days, I firmly told him to take me as his second wife, to be able to have me in his arms. The idea clicked with him, and soon I became his second wife with fan-fare. That was despite opposition from my 'jethani', who wanted to adopt her brother's son for a child.

Thus increasing my influence, I managed to have full control of the household and the family's real estate business. Soon my 'jethani' had to accept me in my new role, as I gave her due respect and began to manage the family business properly. For revival of my education, I engaged a lady teacher, and thus turned the tide in my favour in due course."

"Well, yours is really a story of success in the face of mountainous difficulties. What do you think could be really behind your success?"

"Nothing, but my determination to succeed."

"Do you think, the so-called God or fate also had any role to play in your success?"

"I am not very sure, but more or less I am inclined to believe now, that so-called God with various names and forms as known to the humans, had been conceived by some clever people, to keep the lesser mortals under subjugation. And the so-called fate is really the refuge of those, who are mentally weak. I did not believe all these things, when you told my elder sister and me, many years back. But the practicability of your sermons has since dawned on me and here I am, enjoying the fruits of my determination. Yes, why not?"

"Yes, of course! But, what about the morning 'puja', regular visits to this or that place of worship, and other such things, which took a lot of your time before your transformation?"

"All really useless! Why waste time on all such things which make one dependant on something unknown and impracticable?"

"Marvellous!" He remarked, and asked with a hug, "What about your 'jeth'-turned-husband? Could he physically satisfy you?"

"Not at all. A big failure since the day one. On his part, only satisfied with fondling my body curves, in turn just flaring up my libido. Nothing more. He is, by and large content with his compulsive drinking since allowed by me at home, and sleeping with the two of us turn by turn, of course without causing any flutter on the sexual front. That's the problem. I tried others, but all proved mere duds. Majority were only after my money. Just fond of eating and drinking, but, capable of nothing else! Once I went for a night with three of them. All failed. No match for you. So, keeping myself busy in business, I longed for you to come one day, and here you are!"

After listening to all that Parody had to say, he kissed her forehead, and took to making to-and-fro thrusts with his hip-zone. And under his plough, his ladylove took to making meaningless noises, as an expression of her admiration for the long-desired love play with him.

* * *

Chapter 39

Sapna, his partner-in-adultery of long standing, stood smiling in a kimono, supporting gold-frame spectacles, and carrying a bouquet, when he opened the door on hearing her familiar knock. Her appearance spoke of the 'beauty parlour of repute run by a Japanese woman', where she was working. How nice to see her! Body wise, to say! Looked the same, as she was four years back, but for little flab under the chin. Not only that, she also gave a glimpse of her ardent affection for him by throwing a flying kiss, while handing over the bouquet.

Into the room, he placed aside the bouquet, put his hands underneath her armpits, and kissed her. In turn, she lifted her arms and fell in a tight embrace. She had been told of his arrival that day itself by Parody, before leaving for the airport to catch an Indian Airlines flight to Darjeeling. His conference had ended in the forenoon, and he had been sleeping for quite some time after a hearty lunch, when Sapna came. That very day, he had received a message from his office, conveying the sanction of 40-day leave sought by him, and he had informed his family back home, about his 'decision' to visit his so-called 'old colleagues in the North-East'.

Hugging each other excitedly, they fell on the bed. With their minds racing back to 'the good old days', their bodies felt like wax in a melting pot. It could be a rare repeat of a one-time-freely-available treat. So, with the spirit of 'only now and never hereafter', the goal was to make the maximum of the opportunity. Parody was already on way to Darjeeling, and there was none else to interfere. Thus, the flames of passion rising high, made them begin with their favourite game of 'bed-polo', again after four long years.

With her kimono and under garments thrown away, it was the same Sapna, without even a thread on her body for a cover. Above all, she was in full sensuous glory, straining her limbs to help him keep the two mingling bodies in perfect union. Holding her in a bear hug in perfect nakedness, the debauchee in him was all-gaga! No doubt, the age factor and the past week with Parody were telling upon his drive, but 'the old men are like old wines' they say, 'and the passing time only adds to their flavour and taste'. Moreover, by mid 40s, he had become experienced enough to satisfy a woman as per 'tricks of the trade', laid down in the 'Kamasutra', and there he was, pushing and pulling his sweet heart at a leisure pace.

With the two of them fully immersed in the joy of give and take, no other issue was at stake. The purpose was only to enjoy the life as it was in its 'present' mode. And passing through those blissful moments, the male-pig in him had many questions aimed at gratifying its lustful mind.

"Do you ever remember me?" was his first calculated question.

"Yes very much. And so does Munni! What ever you have done to her!"

"You know, the love begets love, and so does the affection, which I have plenty for her."

"What ever you call it, but I know fully well, my younger sister is almost mad for you. By the way when did you come?"

"Just when you saw me. Why . . . ?"

"Are you kidding?"

"What if I say no?"

"Nothing serious. Otherwise, the servants told me, Munni had met a burly Punjabi in this hotel a few days back and stayed on. Subsequently also, she is known to be visiting this hotel for hours. As per my knowledge, she stayed here overnight as well. Anyhow, the visits could be for business purposes only. The night-stay could be to attend some marriage or a club function. My younger sister is very smart, I tell you. Only the other day she made fifty thousand rupees as commission in a single deal."

"How smart of her! So, both of you have changed your lives for the better." He blurted a bit awkwardly to change the subject, after the subtle revelation.

"Yes, but that is all the result of your sermons. Especially those aimed at improving ones sense of courage to face life boldly."

"When exactly did you feel the change for the better coming your way?" He fired the next question, still a bit perplexed.

"Well, it happened long back. Exactly it began, the day I called you to the bedroom, and insisted on feeding the first spoonful of a tasty dish to you with my own hand. Really, my courage for what I did that day was the result of your assuring sermons. In fact, your protective and rational stance had so emboldened me that come what may, I was fully determined to fall in your arms that day. That was why I was throwing one hint after the other. Do you remember how I sat by your side, covering your leg with my 'ghagra'? Do you remember how I nudged you to help me find my favourite channel on the television without handing over the 'Remote' to you? Do you remember how I placed my forearm on your thigh, pretending to be watching the semi-nude heroine and favourably reacting to the advances of the hero in the song sequence on television? Do you remember how boldly I asked you to prepare tea for me? Do you remember how I encouraged you to place your hands on my shoulders that day? Well, that was my first successful step at making the best use of the 'present', by forgetting the 'past' and the 'future' as per your advice. And there has never been looking back for me since then. Rather I dare say I have never experienced the 'dwindling spirits syndrome' since then. Also, I could find easy solutions to all my problems since then. So much so, I could even get my alcoholic husband cured to lead a normal life."

"Please don't get so sentimental. I have not done anything out of the way for you. May be, what I did was all for selfish motive of bedding you. Otherwise, where else could have I found a willing partner with a sensual and supple body like you, for my sexual fantasies?"

"But for that matter, my sexual needs were more pressing than yours. To what use could have I put my sensual and supple body, with my uninterested husband, and without a desiring and seductive man like you? Nothing more than just wasting myself under the burden of life. Just I tell you, in serving your so-called selfish motive, you have also saved me from ruin. Furthermore, I have never experienced any feelings of guilt in bedding with you. All that we did within the four walls of your flat all those years settled in my mind just as natural activity. To be very frank, I never felt any shame or guilt while disrobing in your presence. Not even at the very first time, when you unhooked my 'choli' at the back and undid the knot of my 'ghagra'. May be I always felt comfortable and assured under your plough. So much so, I have always found your bear hugs, deep bites on the delicate parts of my body and occasional twisting and turning of my limbs, as absolutely enjoyable. Even presently with your maleness inside me, I have the enthusiasm of a longing wife meeting her loving husband after a long time. What ever may be your feelings, my surrender is complete and satisfying to me."

"Thank you for the compliments. Many thanks for the revelation that your surrender is without any guilt. But for change of the subject, would you mind telling me, if I can place your legs on my shoulders now?"

"Sure, sure. You have every right to use this body, the way you like." Sapna said, and asked, "But, what about my favourite, 'on all the fours'?"

"Yes, that is next on agenda and may be more, but that also depends upon the time you can spare for this foray, may be our last."

"No problem at any rate for two nights, after which Munni will be back from Darjeeling. And why do you even visualise this foray becoming the last for us? If you can come all the way to Kolkata, why can't I go all the way to your place in Punjab to meet you there? And my dear, if I am around, I am sure you will certainly spare a night or two, to be able to place my legs on your shoulders in the nude. Say yes!"

"How nice, you have learnt to nourish fond hopes as well!"

"Mind it that was also one of your lessons many years back. To manipulate the available resources with a positive mind for favourable results, I mean. Say yes!"

So, there was none else but the two of them in Kolkata for the two coming nights and the intervening day. There were many items on the agenda. A visit to the famous Victoria Memorial, boating in the port area, bath at the beach and a cabaret show were main attractions. All that was of course besides what they did in the hotel. Meaning tichy-tachy, titsy-bitsy, titter-tatter, tittle-tattle, topsy-turvy and fiddle-faddle! How else would one describe the actions of two lovebirds behind closed doors of a hotel room?

* * *

Chapter 40

Booking for the honeymoon-hut at the hotel near Darjeeling had been arranged through a travel agent. Parody, in a lavish Punjabi bridal-dress as 'newlywed', looked like a 'burning flame' and was in very high spirits, when they checked in the hotel some time in the late afternoon. She had left her son in the care of her former 'jethani' and the maidservant, on the pretext of looking after her 'jeth'-turned-husband in the nature-cure hospital. As they entered the hotel lobby hand in hand, nobody raised an eyebrow despite the difference of two decades in their ages. Even if someone had, they would have cared a hoot, because 'all is fair in love and war' they say.

The well-proportioned and well-behaved receptionist of the hotel warmly welcomed them on entry. Her 'gora-chitta' face very faintly appeared familiar, but he could not immediately make out where he had seen her. Supporting a pair of 'Newport Jeans' and a see-through mini top, with her belly button peeping out like a taxi-driver's face, the receptionist offered them a local made potion to drink, with a prayer for 'happy honeymoon', as per the 'hotel tradition'.

He could recognize the receptionist only while signing the hotel register later, when flashing a mischievous and familiar looking grin she remarked, "So you have married your beautiful Personal Secretary! Whatever could have happened to her previous marriage, as well as yours? Hi . . . Hi . . . ! What do you say?"

Yes, you have guessed rightly. She was the former receptionist of City Hotel near Kolkata Airport, where he had stayed with Parody about four years back.

"Yes, yes, I have married her." He said, a bit awkwardly and asked, "But how come you are here?"

"Mine is a sad story! My husband ditched me, for the slut of a woman more than his age. Bastard! I came here two years back for better emoluments, and so much so to forget my ugly past. By the way, I am taking over as Deputy Manager here, when the present incumbent retires next month."

"I hope you do not feel lonely here!"

"Yes I do. But, life is like that, and I hope to find the merchant of my dreams here one day. Like your Personal Secretary has found. Hi . . . Hi . . . ! What do you say?"

"I have all the good wishes for your success!" He said and hurried to join Parody, who had by then drifted away to see some wall paintings in the huge hotel lobby.

The exclusive honeymoon-hut of the hotel was perched on a mound. It was a honeymoon-hut in the real sense, away from the main building. There was absolutely no interference of any kind, except the pre-fixed visits of the polite-speaking and smartly dressed staff members, always moving in pairs, for catering and maintenance. There were in fact, about half a dozen such huts, at considerable distance from each other, scattered along the periphery of the sprawling hotel grounds, which covered a vast plateau. The rugged landscape of the plateau dotted with rocky mounds was lush-green with a rich variety of flora. Zigzagged by stone-lined pathways, the hotel grounds were secured with a perimeter-wall, topped by Y-shaped barbed wire fencing like a prisoners-of-war camp. There was regular patrolling by the hotel guards on an all-season track along the perimeter-wall. In addition, there was a foolproof alarm system in place, and no harm could come to the lodgers from any side.

Beyond the particular hut, the plateau abruptly ended with a steep rocky face lowering into a mighty rivulet, across which was dense jungle, abounding in wild animals, notably the elephants. Binoculars were available for watching the jungle scene from the security of the hut.

The structure of the hut was an architectural wonder. It was artistically built on a round platform supported by five concrete pillars. The pillars stood in a tank, filled with water for swimming. A pathway, fortified by an 8-feet wall, surrounded the tank. The wooden staircase leading from the ground to the main platform was so designed; it was mechanically lifted at night to provide a sense of security to the occupants of the hut. The well furnished main room with a double bed at the centre had big mirrors on all the four walls and the roof, whereby one could see for sure, ones reflections of what ever one did in the room at any given time. The bath-cum-dressing room, side-room and drawing-cum-dining room, were also tastefully furnished. There was a 12-feet wide 'veranda' surrounding the dwelling unit with big windows all around, having see-through glass-panes covered with lavish curtains. To top it all, there was a big canopy upstairs. The canopy was so built that there could be absolutely no interference from sun and rain. The chances of success for the Peeping Tom if any were completely ruled out. Then there was a flawlessly regular supply of consumables including cooked food for the 'honeymooning couple' to serve and win everlasting admiration of each other. What a nice place it was, to live and understand each other, far from the madding crowds!

By the virtue of its far-away location, the hotel in fact was home to those who wanted to pass some carefree time away from the humdrum life of cut-throat competitions. The hotel occupancy was almost hundred percent and at any given time from dusk to dawn, one found people of all sizes and shapes trudging the winding pathways or relaxing here and there, unmindful of the life around. The area being rain-prone, a good number of rain-shelters existed all over the hotel grounds.

Reaching the honeymoon-hut, they were ushered into the drawing room by a pair of smart maidservants. After serving them with 'welcome sweets' and cold drinks, they took Parody round the hut, explaining self-service in respect of food etc. Their job done, the maidservants went away, leaving the two of them alone.

There had been a gap of almost two days and one night since his last go with Sapna, giving sufficient time and energy to his body and mind to cast lustful eyes on Parody in bridal dress. But, the courtesy demanded of him, to wait for the formal 'suhagraat' to commence after dinner. Therefore, after the maids left, he just followed his 'bride' on a familiarity round of the hut. The hut itself being matchless in design and decorations, the best view of the surroundings was available from the canopy. The panoramic view all around, gave a feel of nature in its full splendour. The settings were just eye-catching.

* * *

Chapter 41

After a round of the hut, Parody suggested, they sit in the canopy for some time, which seemed to be at the top of the world, from where even the main hotel building was at a lower level. The idea was appreciable, and he settled on an easy chair in an anticipating mood. Sensing his mood, as an Indian bride is expected to; Parody went downstairs and soon returned with a beer can, along with a mug and some snacks. Then, making herself comfortable in the easy chair in front of him, she poured beer, and formally invited him to lift the mug. Encased by the red 'dupatta', her face exuded trance-like aura. Her sleepy slanting eyes had the submission of a village belle bedecked to meet her groom on the 'suhagraat'.

Briefly looking into his eyes while pouring the drink, Parody shot a streak of yearning, which he had never experienced before. Happy at the turn of events and bringing the beer mug to the height of her face, he proposed a toast 'for our extended honeymoon'. Then taking two big sips, he handed the mug over to Parody to follow. So, enjoying the commencement of the 'honeymoon', sipping beer from the same mug turn by turn, they sat there until late evening, and went downstairs.

After a bath followed by lazy dinner, he sat before the television to catch up with the latest on the Indian news front, littered with various scams and the brave efforts of the 'conglomerate in power' headed by an 'oldhead' in Delhi, to remain in power in the face of the pranks of the alliance partners like Mamta, Lalu Yadav etc. Meanwhile, his 'bride' cleared the dining table and went to the bedroom unnoticed.

Entering the bedroom after listening to the Aaj Tak, Star, and Zee news bulletins, he found Parody in 'ghungat' standing near the door with folded hands. As soon as he entered, she touched his feet and stood in silence. Watching her action, his heart became heavy with feelings of love for her, and just lifting her bodily, he took her to the bed.

However, he felt they were not alone in the bedroom and had company! Yes, as he moved towards the bed lifting Parody, their reflections also moved accordingly in the surrounding mirrors. How nice to see ones own actions on 'suhagraat'! Only the one knows better, who has lived the experience!

Making Parody sit on the bed, he lifted her 'ghungat', only to find her in tears. Anyhow, completing the ceremony, he gave her a five hundred-rupee note as 'ghungat-uthai' and kissed her forehead. Then unable to control his curiosity at her tears any more, he lifted her chin and blurted, "What is this?"

"May be, these are tears of my happiness at having you at last as I wished." Parody said, and asked between sobs, "Do you know, how deeply I am in love with you?"

"Yes, your elder sister also told me so, but why to weep at this juncture of happiness?"

"May be you will not appreciate my feelings. I wonder if all men are the same!"

"No. Not at all! It is not like that. I appreciate your feelings very much!"

"How do I know?"

"Why should I be here at all, if I had no love for you?"

"Would you continue loving me so for ever?"

"Yes, but who told you, I will not?"

"May be it is just my illusion. May be I am just afraid of loosing you. Please don't mind my tears."

"Don't be silly so as to think like that. Come on now give me a smile. And what about giving me the honeymoon ride as well? Quick!"

"What is the honeymoon ride? Do I have to carry you on my back? I have never heard of it before."

"No, you are not to carry me on your back. But, the ride it surely is. And as per the custom in Punjab, you can claim to be my better half, only after giving me the honeymoon ride. Understand?"

"Yes, but how do I give you the ride, to claim to be your better half?"

"Very simple if you agree and follow what I say."

"Yes, I agree! Tell me what to do now."

"Okay, no more questions please. Ready?"

"Yes, I am ready to follow!"

"Well, no disobeying now. Simply follow what I say. Yes, take off all your clothes one by one."

"Hmm . . . Well . . . Here goes 'dupatta' . . . Oonh . . . Oonh . . . and . . . here goes . . . the 'kameez' . . . and the . . . bra . . . Okay?"

"Well done! Well done! How beautiful, you my love! Your breasts are desirable! Take out the 'salwar' now. Yes . . . Yes . . . Throw it away and take out the underwear. Good . . . Good . . . My beautiful bride . . . !"

Having thus got Parody disrobed, he took her in a hug, and adjusted his middle part between her thighs, with a pillow under her hips. Then with a kiss on her lips, he inserted the head of his male shaft into her vaginal cavity, and asked, "Ready for the ride?"

"Very clever of you!" She muttered, and encircled his thighs with her legs; in a way accompanying him to the realm of sensual reality as he passionately forced the entry.

"Tell me now. How much love do you have for me?" He asked, giving forward jerks to his hip-zone.

"Too much. Really. Whole of me for you . . . and for ever!"

"What do you mean by 'whole of me'?"

"Every thing. I mean my 'tan, man, dhan'".

"Right. All right. But for now, I am satisfied only with your 'whole' without 'w'".

"Yes my chosen rider, that is already at your disposal. No doubt. But, why only my 'whole' without 'w'? I am at a loss to know! Say yes!"

"That is the priority just now my love!"

"Well, well, my burly rider! Do not be short sighted enough, just to be satisfied with my 'whole' without 'w'. May be, only for your own sake, you should open your third eye. The eye of your prolific mind I mean. My 'whole' at your disposal, includes my 'whole' without 'w' as well. Further, my 'whole' without 'w' may be of no use to your 'whole self' unless you put 'whole' of me in your 'whole' use. Say yes!"

"So nice of you for guidance. But, what about placing your legs on my shoulders for a proper ride?"

"Also included in my 'whole' self. Why seek permission?"

So, with Parody's blanket permission, he went the whole hog, to satisfy his passionate mind, in the act making her issue the shrieks of sexual indulgence.

There was no hurry and worry. Their relationship had the guise of 'honeymoon'. The surrender of Parody was complete, and both of them were in a mood to oblige. There was none else in the exclusive honeymoon-hut except the two of them, and so there was no need to speak in hushed voices. The desire ruled supreme and the longing partners of the love game had no other distraction except their reflections in the surrounding mirrors. The prevailing sound other than their intermittent hissing was only 'futch . . . futch'.

The 'she' in Parody had willingly bared herself, for his 'height' to measure her 'depth', and the male-pig in him was at its favourite pursuit. What more could have he wished? Virtually nothing! Agree with me? Yes or no?

* * *

Chapter 42

For full five weeks from that night onward, they lived in that exclusive hut as newlyweds. For health sake, he taught a few yoga and acupressure exercises to Parody, which she obediently performed after morning-walk every day, along with him. There was absolutely no place in their daily life for religion or what the people call God, because like him, realising the futility of belief in the rigmarole of the things religious, Parody had also understood the power of mind, and the need to develop it for happy living. For that matter, she properly learnt to adopt 'shavasan' after yoga and acupressure every morning, and to repeat his 'mantra' of the mind: I am the master of myself and determined to enjoy a healthy wealthy and problem-free life with self-help.

As a matter of routine, they spent better part of the day, under the spacious canopy. It was usually in the nude or semi-nude. They settled downstairs after the evening bath for dinner to the accompaniment of music and news on television. More often than not, they also frolicked in the water tank below the hut for an hour or so in the evening, where he gave swimming lessons to Parody, before the visit of catering-staff. Always after the dinner, they took a leisurely stroll in the circular veranda, after which it was time to bed.

Before mounting the bed however, they indulged in foreplay igniting the fires of passion in each other. That was followed by a prolonged spell of copulation before falling into sound sleep by midnight. Then getting up by sunrise, they began their day with fresh fruit juice after morning ablutions, and thereafter skipping breakfast, they took brunch. After the brunch, they slept upstairs for about two hours, followed by reading, gossiping or just lazing about.

While reclining on the easy chair under the canopy, it was always an enjoyable treat for him, to hold Parody in the nude like a child in his lap, and move his fingers timelessly, on her back and through her hair. So lying motionless on to him, with closed eyes as if in sleep, she allowed his aura to mingle with hers and make them feel like one body and one mind.

Parody went thrice to Kolkata by air, during the 'honeymoon', to see her son and the business. Once a week, she went to stay overnight with her 'jeth'-turned-husband in the nature cure hospital about 50 kms away. That gave ample time to his body to recharge itself with passionate energy required for the bed-games.

The period crucial to Parody becoming the mother of his second child, commenced on the day she returned after two nights from her first visit to Kolkata. On return that late afternoon, she looked dazzling in a costly kimono, and exuded happiness. The 'realization' came to him, when he kissed her in welcome, and found her body temperature as slightly more than normal. Later, reclining onto an easy chair under the canopy, she delighted him with stories of her son for long. Listening spellbound to her, he felt enchanted with her inner and outer beauty, all the time rejoicing at the anticipation of impregnating her that night or the next. How nice he felt at being able to read the signal of her mature egg cell waiting in the depths of her body, for one of his sperms! The thought occupied his mind throughout the evening and to his dismay, the night appeared to be unusually delaying its arrival while the intermittent rain added fire to the fuel of his passion.

Eventually, during the last round of the after-dinner stroll in the surrounding veranda, it was time for him to put his hand passionately on Parody's waist. With her positive response, he took her in a tight embrace and moving his hands on her back down to sturdy hips, he planted kisses on her neck and face. All over her body, he found the 'symptom' loud and clear. So, his 'bride' was 'in heat' in the real sense that night; fully prepared to receive his seed, and nurture it to grow into a human being full of hope, courage, and many other possibilities. Her 'preparedness' also fully registered itself on his conscience, when holding her hips he realised she was not wearing any under garment with kimono.

As it was already time to go the whole hog, he guided Parody straight to the bedroom, all along twitching her sensual nipples. By the time they approached the bed, she hastily threw away her kimono and admiringly caught hold of his male organ with both hands. That reminded him of a statue seen somewhere in a western country. Anyhow, her action appeared to be the result of a doze of 'kajufeni', taken in celebration of her happy return from Kolkata that day. Thinking so, he helped her mount the bed and hinted to adopt 'on all the fours' position. As she placed her parted knees on the edge of the bed and took the desired position, he slightly patted her buttocks and upper back, and guided the head of his male shaft into her vaginal orifice, from her backside. Then, cupping her breasts with his hands, he adjusted the proper angle and sent in the whole shaft with slow hip-jerks, to which she responded with sensual grunts at a high pitch. However, soon he made her change over to the usual 'sprawl' with a pillow under her hips; to put her at the receiving end with no holds barred.

* * *

Chapter 43

An abrasion occurred during the third visit of Parody to Kolkata. It commenced when he went to the main hotel building to while away the time. There he found the bewitching receptionist and went to say "Hello" to her!

"Hello!" She responded, and offered a seat.

"Thanks!" He said taking the seat, and asked, "How's life going on?"

"At a snail's pace exactly for me. But I gather you are going very strong with your 'honeymoon'. Hi . . . Hi! What do you say?"

"Yes! But, who told you?"

"Why? Your secretary-turned-bride of course! I can read from her bubbling face very well, every time I see her. She exuded a lot of positive signals, when she told me today morning that she was going to Kolkata, and would be back day after tomorrow only".

"So, you seem to be an expert at behavioural sciences as well! I presume you have picked up the expertise in your day to day public dealings in the hotel business!"

"Just by the way. I have an irritating question to ask you. Have you really married her?"

"May be, a sort of . . . You may call it a marriage of convenience if you like."

"Convenience for you or her?"

"May be it is for both. Though it may be for varying reasons. That is."

"What do you mean by 'varying reasons'?"

"Yes, varying reasons for me and her. For me it is passion and for her it is her obsession for me out of compulsion. That is!"

"That no doubt makes some sense. After all, I cannot go wrong. Hi . . . Hi! What do you say?"

"So, you can read between the lines as well. But, why have you never cared to visit us in our hut?"

"Well, I wanted to . . . But, I did not want to . . . I mean . . . disturb you. No harm in coming if you invite. Hi . . . Hi! What do you say?"

"What if I invite you in the absence of my bride?"

"No problem. But, I will be free from here only by evening while tomorrow is my rest day."

"Do I invite you for a lazy dinner tonight in that case?"

"Sure, sure! But you know the people generally make a mountain of the molehill. Hi . . . Hi! What do you say?"

"Yes, you are right. But, in that case we can strive to keep the visit secret if you agree."

"How can that be possible on earth? I am very well known here."

"Why can't you pretend to be on a late evening walk and drop in after the visit of the catering-staff, and stay for the night to slip away any time tomorrow?"

"Yes, but that depends."

"Depends . . . what?"

"The secrecy and the night stay I mean."

"I don't get you!"

"Okay, I come. Forget the depending part."

"So nice of you!" He said and buzzed off.

Her name was Komal, the delicate, and she turned out to be a half-Punjaban. That, she was to tell him later that night. Her 'background' was curvaceous and supple enough like her body. Her mother, Kamini, was born in a Punjabi family settled for business in Ahmedabad, Gujarat. Kamini was brought up in an atmosphere, whereby her 'liberated' parents used to attend the famous 'Guchha Parties'.

Well, 'Guchha Parties' are nothing but a ritual, encompassing wife swapping for the sake of 'novelty' in sexual enjoyment. As every married person realises, after 10/12 years of married life and bearing a couple of children, the craving for 'new' sex partner germinates in the human mind. Biologically speaking, the male dominates the sex act to produce offspring in most of the mammals and so in humans. This domination is so all pervading that every male wants more than one female for sex act, even sometimes in the face of fatal consequences. Like animals, the urge for more and more females for sex act exists among humans as well. It is like Microsoft Windows 'default'. As human societies the world over are 'customized' and traumatized by some religious, social and legal sanctions, this 'default action' by and large remains inactive. Therefore, most of the human males more or less have to remain content with their respective 'life partners', but the known human history is also replete with the instances of the urge for 'new' raising its head as a 'default' in every society. While the 'high and mighty' are known to openly fulfil this urge under one pretext or the other, the lesser mortals generally adopt the dubious and pretentious methods like the 'Guchha Parties'. The beauty of the whole thing is that playing the passive role through ages, the female of the human specie has also developed the craving for 'new' though passively.

To bring home the point, let us thankfully quote Barbara Ellen, where she highlights the 'terrible design fault in men' showing 'their contempt for the familiar' and 'infatuation with the new'. As per Barbara, every 'wise woman knows that she can be everything in the world to her partner, but, she cannot be new'. Further, 'the wiser woman also knows that trying too hard to appear fresh and new just makes her silly and paranoid'. However, the learned Barbara also feels the urge of 'the woman' for 'new', but, according to her, the woman feels more 'besotted by the way someone treats her as new' than being 'attracted by the new'. Still further, 'when a woman has had a long time of being taken for granted by her partner, and feels placed in importance somewhere below his need for clean socks, it can be tantalizing to be found interesting again'. Furthermore, 'women have been known to throw away relationship of many years' standing', just to feel 'fascinating, mysterious, enchanting, amusing and new' again.

So, some people in Gujarat seem to have invented the 'Guchha Party' out of their urge for 'new'. As per the known practice, invitations, telephonic or otherwise, are sent to the 'member couples only' for this or that 'party'. After an evening of eating, drinking and dancing, the car keys of the invitees are placed in a bunch (Guchha) in a dark corner. One by one come the departing women, to lift a key ring each at random, and sit in the particular car. Then come the men to take home a 'new' woman each. After a night of fulfilment, an exercise is undertaken early next morning to drop home the 'new lilies'. How dubious and pretentious, but enchanting! Wife swapping in India!

In those environs, Komal's mother Kamini had found her match in a Bihari Babu, Shiv Shankar Manjhi, and eloped to make a home with him. The relationship was accepted by her 'liberated' parents without any hitch and everything went on very well till the euphoria of 'youthful adventure' lasted and boredom of familiarity set in. Living in Dehradun, the queen of hills, the Bihari Babu one day found his wife, Kamini, in compromising position with his boss in the tea-estate where he was employed. However, instead of becoming furious, he simply allowed his wife to live with his boss and himself shifted to another tea-estate along with his adolescent daughter, Komal. Soon thereafter, the climax came when he brought home the estranged wife of his erstwhile 'unfaithful' boss. The stepmother herself a story of parental apathy, treated Komal nicely. As the years rolled by, Komal became youthful enough to find a match for her. She had by then armed herself with an MBA degree. She married the prince of her dreams, a Bengali, and went to live with him in Kolkata, where our main character had seen her for the first time working as a hotel receptionist. How befittingly someone has said, 'Potatoes and Punjabis are found every where!

*   *   *

Chapter 44

Komal came to his hut in pouring rain that late evening, soon after the visit of the catering staff. For the sake of disguise, she had put on an ample raincoat with a wide hat. She arrived like a weary traveller, carrying a bag and a walking stick. Waiting anxiously for her by that time, he had placed a 'kajufeni' bottle and two glasses on the table, along with an assortment of dry fruits.

Receiving the guest downstairs, he accompanied her to the drawing-cum-dining room, and returned to mechanically lift the staircase for the night. When he re-entered after some time, there was a pleasant surprise! His guest had changed over to a red & blue dress of Arabian belly dancers and was pouring 'kajufeni'.

"I thought of saving on time while you were busy! Hi . . . Hi! What do you say?"

"Very nice . . . Very nice! But, why save on time? Are you not staying over?"

"Of course! Of course!! But you know it is always good to economise on time. You know the time is the most precious gift of nature to the humankind. Hi . . . Hi! What do you say?"

"How lucky for me to have a guest, who is two-in-one. Beauty and philosophy, I mean!" He said and sat down by her side on the sofa.

Lifting the glasses, they discussed 'the weather' during first round and changed over to 'the purpose of human life' during the second. As the weather was 'just lovely' and the 'purpose of life' boiled down to 'just an effort at give and take of happiness with malice towards none', the third round saw them changing glasses after every sip and 'unintentionally' nudging each other. The fourth round they made 'lovely' and finished along with the 'lazy dinner', following which they ventured out to the circular veranda for a symbolic walk.

Taking the symbolic walk, soon they entered the twilight zone of 'let's have it', where by he became 'brave enough' to guide the obliging guest by the waist to the bedroom and make her sit on an edge of the bed, with her legs dangling on a side.

While she was sitting motionless, her red & blue dress tried in vain to shield her body curves from his passionate eyes. Her black and fragrant hair encasing her oval face cascaded downward as if flirting with her well-rounded balls of breasts. As he placed his hands on her shoulders, there was that proverbial resistance of the Indian woman on her part, actually giving the go-ahead. So, taking her resistance in his stride, he kissed her for the first time, expressing the desire to have her urgently . . . for what she had come. As she reciprocated passionately, he took to fumbling with her dress to disrobe her, without any resistance. And soon there after, their bodies fused with each other and uninhibited noises of sexual play began issuing from the secluded hut, which of course were muffled by the rain and had no listener other than the two of them. With the surrounding mirrors dutifully reflecting the actions of the copulating couple, the panorama was worth being video-graphed, while nobody knows how it ended that night!

When he woke up next morning, he found Komal by his side in sleep without even a string on her well-preserved and shapely body, which had his teeth marks at vulnerable places. Then he heard a ring familiar with the catering-staff. Without waking up the sleeping beauty, he tiptoed to the window to wave away the catering-staff with a 'not required' gesture, and went to the bedroom again to feast his eyes. Sitting on the downside of the bed, he realised the aura of satisfaction playing on the sleeping damsel's face. She was more or less in a sprawl. Her face was slightly turned right, with arms parallel to the torso as in 'shavasan'. Her shapely legs were stretched, with the exception that the left leg was slightly bent upward, and the knee raised consequently, was tilted over to the right leg. In totality, the chubby hemispheres of her breasts were going up and down rhythmically, in accordance with the rise and fall of her vertebra resulting from her slow breathing. What more, her luxuriant hair was lying in a crushed heap beside her head.

* * *

Chapter 45

Since gone are the days, when he fulfilled the desire of Parody 'to get lost some where' along with him.

Since gone are the days when he lived with Parody in that exclusive hut, and had ample time to 'stand and stare' at her, free from the anxieties of life.

Since gone are the days when he could hold Parody, in flesh and blood, the way he liked.

Since gone are the days, when Parody in the nude, used to sit in front of him in various poses, giving a fascinating view of her body contours from all conceivable angles.

Since gone are the days, when Parody in the nude or semi-nude remained glued to him, day in and day out.

Since gone are the days, when he used to play hide and seek with naked Parody in that exclusive hut.

Since gone are the days, when he used to have joint baths with Parody: under the shower, in the big bathtub and in the tank below the hut.

Since gone are the days, when he held Parody with her bare breasts pressed against his chest and her warm breath blowing on to his face, unhindered for long spells of time.

Since gone are the days, when Parody felt more comfortable in the nude or semi-nude in his presence, than in clothes.

Since gone are the days, when his every night with Parody was 'suhagraat'.

Since gone are the days, when he gave to the female in Parody, what she wanted from the male in him.

Since gone are the days, when the chauvinistic male-pig in him got what it wanted from the female in Parody.

Since gone are the days, when Parody used to issue loud shrieks of blissful enjoyment, in tune with his repeated male thrusts.

Since gone are the days, when he gave another chip off his block to Parody.

Since gone are the days, when at the end of prolonged copulation by mid-night, Parody used to snuggle into his hold for a sound sleep, in the nude.

It was during those days, when scanning the far side of the mighty rivulet through binoculars from the canopy one afternoon, Parody, prompted him to watch what she had spotted. There were three elephants frolicking along the far side of the rivulet. One of them was a heavyweight male, and two females. The females, one old and big, and the other young and small, could be mother and daughter. The burly male was in the process of mounting the smaller female, when he went to the 'scene'. As he stood behind Parody and focussed his binoculars in the pointed direction, he found the male elephant in action; with his mighty forelegs possessively clutching the belly of the cute female, half his size, while the older female appeared to be interfering in awe. The next moment, not caring about the presence of the older female, the bull moved his hind legs closer to his mount, and with a groping pause, gave a forceful thrust. Thus, the whole of elephant's male organ went tearing into the female's aspiring slit, like a piston, causing imbalance enough for her to fall on fore-knees. As the lovers disengaged after the action, the male stood motionless with his limp member dangling harmlessly, while the cute little female turning her face towards him, began caressing his head with her trunk, as if to get him ready for a re-take.

The scene was the rarest of rare, but by that time, Parody became sentimental and taking him in a tight embrace with her face buried into his chest, she blurted, "Stop. Stop. Don't see. Don't see."

Astonished, he took her away from the scene, and asked, "What happened?"

Her reply was in the form of a question, "What if somebody watches us, the same way?"

That was really convincing, and appreciating her sentiments, he took to kissing her feverishly.

Discussing the event that night during love play, Parody pointed out what she described as a 'striking similarity' of their physical dimensions as compared to those of the mating elephant couple. Really, a monster like him was the male elephant, and what a cute little thing was the female, like Parody!

"What about the bigger female?" He asked.

"Kabab ki haddi! May be like my sister!!" Parody replied, and buried her face into his chest.

* * *

Chapter 46

After the carefree 'honeymoon' in that wonderfully secluded hut, they left by the Darjeeling-Kolkata-Delhi-Chandigarh flight of Indian Airlines one evening. They were very sure by then, of Parody returning with a fertilized egg cell in her womb, as she had since missed her 'monthly'. On his part, he was returning with the fulfilment of a whimsical wish on the amorous side of his life. As they had done ample talking all those days, nothing much transpired between them during the flight.

Only question Parody asked during the whole journey was, "When do you intend to see us again?"

To her question, his reply was, "When ever you really wish."

Then there was the last minute dialogue as the plane touched down at Kolkata airport, where Parody had to disembark.

"A very happy journey homeward my dear!" Parody almost sang into his ear, while unbuckling her seat belt.

"But you haven't told me . . . ! Have you forgotten?" He reminded her.

"Nope. I remember. I have to tell you, why I ran away when you kissed me some days before my marriage."

"Why . . . ? I would like to know."

"Because, I knew fully well all along. You were the island of bliss for my elder sister in the desert of her life. Therefore,

I did not want to encroach upon her domain. And in case you intend to deny, I may also tell you how I had once secretly watched the two of you in action. That was some days after you saw me off guards in your bathroom. Yes, why not?"

"So you knew! But, what made you ultimately . . . despite that?"

"Vengeance! Vendetta! Against my elder sister of course! For selecting an impotent groom for me! Moreover, I was in a hurry after my groom's failure to consummate the marriage, and you were the best choice under the given circumstances. Yes, why not?"

"O, I see . . . !" He blurted, almost aghast at the revelation.

"This is not the end." She said and added, "My sister knows everything about what you and me have been up to. Including my first night with you following the farewell dinner you gave me. Also when you saw me under the shower for the first time and when you kissed me some days before my marriage. Yes, why not?"

"And I may tell you more . . . ! That mischievous Punjaban has told me too about her foray with you in my absence. And . . . and how Rachni and Leela became successful with 31-day 'Puja' at the so called 'Temple of Fertility" while staying with you, is also known to me and my sister . . . Please do not mind the disclosures at all. In fact, I am proud of you. Yes, why not?" Parody said, and mingled with the disembarking passengers.

"What a parody!" He remarked and reclined on his seat to wait for the homeward take off; leaving behind his trail of sensuality in the unwieldy India. For the time being at least!

*   *   **The End**   *   *

www.ingramcontent.com/pod-product-compliance
Ingram Content Group UK Ltd.
Pitfield, Milton Keynes, MK11 3LW, UK
UKHW040015200726
13854UKWH00001B/204

9 781456 782979